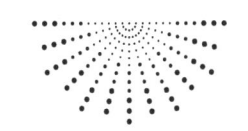

THE LABYRINTH'S ARCHIVIST

THE LABYRINTH'S ARCHIVIST

A BROKEN CITIES NOVELLA

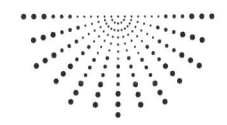

DAY AL-MOHAMED

Copyright © 2019 by Day Al-Mohamed

Cover by S.H. Roddey

All rights reserved.

No part of this book may be reproduced in any form or by any electronic or mechanical means, including information storage and retrieval systems, without written permission from the author, except for the use of brief quotations in a book review.

This book is a work of fiction. Any resemblance to any person, living or dead, is coincidental.

To my wife, Renee, who puts up with me, reads everything I write, and always, always reminds me of what we promised each other: To continuously strive to be better people.

raises a glass

To Better People!

THE LABYRINTH'S ARCHIVIST

Azulea could smell grilled meat from Tamir's stall in the souq abutting the Archive. Her stomach rumbled, reminding her that she'd skipped the midday meal in her nervousness.

The Grand Parlor was a large, loud room, filled with travelers and traders, merchants, and even a few scoundrels. It was a place for them all to relax from their journeys, imbibe beverages from a multitude of worlds, and eat large quantities of wholesome (if not extravagant) meals while swapping lies about adventures and dangers they had faced while traversing the Labyrinth. The hard stone floor and high ceiling let sound billow and rebound off the walls in a way that even the thick woven rugs could not prevent. The sound spilled out the retractable front wall that was wide open to encourage airflow through the building during the heavy heat of this summer afternoon.

The Grand Parlor was not a suitable location to host an informative interview about the Labyrinth. It was too crowded and too public. Yet, here she was. Azulea asked Mosa to repeat what he had just said. Again. For the fourth time. The guttural rumblings and high-pitched squeals of the

Lacerti language, spoken through a face full of sharp teeth, weren't natural to a human larynx. After only ten minutes of speaking it, Azulea's throat was already raw.

The strange, reclusive lizard-men had not visited the Archive in her lifetime, and Azulea knew of only a handful of people who were fluent. She was fortunate that her gift allowed her to learn languages easily. Azulea never forgot anything—every word, every sound, every smell. It was as if things were burned into her brain, or shelved in a library. She just had to think hard enough to retrieve the memory. *Grandmother, I am grateful you made me study so hard, even the "forgotten" languages,* she thought with a flare of warmth before returning her focus to the room.

Azulea knew better, but she gambled that the Grand Parlor would still meet their interview needs. She had asked the Lacerti trader to meet with her, hoping he could bring her information the Archive didn't have. He was scheduled to leave the following morning with a caravan, and his travels through the Labyrinth included fringe worlds of which the Archive knew little. It wasn't protocol, but it was an opportunity too good to miss.

This would be a coup if she could capture new information. Peny, Azulea's cousin, sat next to her, acting as scribe. Peny was terrible at languages. She could write faster than most people could speak, but when it came to speaking other languages herself, Peny rarely got past basic greetings…and the dirty words. Yet together, as a team, they were able to operate as full Archivists. Azulea only hoped this would finally prove their worth and wouldn't lead to yet more heartache. They needed this to be a success.

Mosa's voice was a gargling rumble. Azulea translated. "It was only on the second night when the flapping of leathery wings came down. Claws scraped against the hides of our tents. Hundreds of tiny bodies battered against our shelter. Outside, our mounts screamed as they were devoured."

She could hear Peny. The younger woman kept moving: fidgeting, pulling her hair and swinging feet that didn't quite reach the floor. Despite the bright daylight streaming in and Peny's nearness, Azulea's damaged eyes didn't allow her to see Peny's form clearly. She was just a shadowy splash of color with bright yellow hair.

Azulea ground her teeth. Her cousin was probably ogling the crowd. She was known amongst the trainees for her roving eye and her less-than-discriminating tastes when it came to choices in bed-partners. Azulea remembered too well the many nights when she had lain awake listening to Peny's noisy lovemaking. They had been young students then, sharing a room. That was before, when Azulea still believed that she'd be allowed to become an Archivist despite her blindness.

"Peny, focus," Azulea snapped. She couldn't see what had caught the other woman's attention, but it definitely wasn't on the conversation with Mosa.

"Khun exurendi bharthrar, Mosa." The words were a bark of sound in the Lacerti language. Azulea translated without thinking. *City killer.*

Azulea's head whipped toward the speaker. It came from someone standing a few feet from their table. She couldn't see him, but she recognized the voice. It belonged to Davarr, a merchant from Elishia. He had a tendency toward boastfulness and was not always detailed and accurate with his accountings. His slipshod advice had never gotten anyone harmed…yet. And now he had just publicly called Mosa a killer.

Mosa stood so abruptly that his chair rocked with the violence.

"No, I'm sure he didn't mean that!" Azulea said to the

Lacerti. The syllables were rough, staccato gulps of sound that clearly rang out through the parlor. Even if no one understood the language, what was happening was clear to everyone.

Words filled Azulea's mind from classes and books read to her years ago. *The Lacerti are a fierce and proud people. Rage smolders in their chest like a hearth of burning fire and living flame runs through their veins. Their bodies have been known to reach temperatures high enough to ignite paper. Archivists should proceed with caution.* She had to do something.

Azulea stood and took a step forward. She could feel heat radiating from Mosa, who became noticeably warmer than her own human body. She now understood why they had referred to the Lacerti as the Children of the Sun. She didn't touch Mosa but held her hands up in front of her, palms facing him in a non-threatening gesture, her movements slow and intent.

When two people are getting ready to fight, they face each other, staring into each other's eyes, bodies posturing. The sentence flew through Azulea's mind. She couldn't remember where she had learned it, but she was grateful for the memory. *Put your body between them during this early stage, and you can break the tension.*

She could feel the Lacerti's muscles tighten through the boards of the floor as he shifted his weight. The air around him wavered as the heat from his body increased. Sweat beaded on Azulea's skin. Was he going to attack? She continued, more softly. "Think about what you're doing."

She heard Peny behind her, moving toward the Elishian, Davarr. Perhaps together they could stop the fight before it ever began. She was pretty sure that Davarr spoke Trade.

Azulea continued. "Please, Mosa, this is my first official interview. I really want to do well." The lie slid easily from Azulea's tongue. She shamelessly continued. "My grandmother is ill." Another lie. The interview had been her grandmother's idea. Of course, the old woman would kill Azulea herself if she knew Azulea had attempted an interview in a public setting like the Grand Parlor—the distractions, the noise, and sometimes, unpleasant interruptions—it was always a staggering cacophony of travelers, all day and all night.

Azulea tried to look vulnerable. "Please. I don't need a fight."

Mosa was large, even for a Lacerti. Azulea's head barely came even with his midsection. His reptilian head with its massive jaws curled high over her head, a shadow just beyond the range of her limited sight. She could smell the heavy wool of his kaunakes as the drape warmed against his body.

Silence spread around them like a wave, rushing toward the ends of the room as more and more travelers noticed the commotion. The clink of glasses and murmurs of conversation ceased. Where was the barman? The servers? Azulea's mouth was dry, and her stomach churned.

Behind her, Peny's voice was an unintelligible murmur as she attempted to talk down Davarr.

Azulea heard the rattle of the Elishian's gills. Whatever Peny was saying, it wasn't working. Azulea remembered the description of those gills from her sessions with the Head Archivist. They were an evolution that allowed the Elishians to live in their swampy world. When threatened, they could flutter them quickly and flare them out around their neck, like a great fan, to frighten away predators. It was a sign of threat.

Azulea turned her head toward the Elishian, slipping much more smoothly into his musical sing-song language. "Davarr, this is Mosa's interview. This is not the time, nor place, for your opinion." She stressed the "your."

Davarr's gills rattled again. "We all know about the Lacerti. Destroyers of villages. Burners of worlds." This time he repeated his words in Trade. Davarr clearly wanted everyone to understand him.

Azulea swore internally.

Mosa huffed, hot breath bursting out of him like one of the tiny steam machines that had been brought to the Archive from one of the more technological worlds. "He calls me destroyer, he insults my people, and you ask me to forget? I could burn him up. Like ashes on the air." The words were hissed and rumbled. Azulea winced, hoping that no one understood his words. The Lacerti were already viewed with mistrust by many who traveled the Labyrinth. She didn't need Mosa's threats making things worse.

Fine. If the men wanted to bluster, then she could do the same. "Killer, not killer, your fight has no place inside these walls," Azulea said firmly in Lacerti.

Azulea switched languages again, this time to Trade. Azulea raised her voice so it carried across the parlor. "Whatever your problems are with each other, it does not enter the Residence. We are sanctuary ground."

She repeated the words in Trade and then let her hands drop. She took a step to the left; her soft sandals made little sound on the thick woven mats covering the floor. Azulea now stood squarely between the two potential combatants. She straightened her back and put her hands on her hips, using every ounce of confidence she had. "This is finished, or you can both continue outside the Residence," she paused, "and outside the Archive." She raised her hand in the direction of the doorway. It was a threat, and when making a threat, a little drama never hurt.

There were travelers who walked the Labyrinth who preferred to keep their secrets, but many knew and understood the value of the Archive and the role of the Archivists.

Their maps were prized, and their information and attention to detail ensured that merchants and traders were able to make cross-world travel less dangerous and more profitable. Everybody won.

To be threatened with losing access to the Archive was serious. Fighting or threatening the safety of anyone in the Archive was an automatic banishment. The only way the Residence worked was for all those who stayed within to feel secure.

Azulea wasn't sure she even had the authority for a banishment; after all, she wasn't a real Archivist. They said she could never be a full Archivist because of her eyes. She quickly squelched the thought. Now was not the time for self pity.

Azulea felt a presence slide up beside her. The scent of musky persimmon filled her nostrils. It was Peny. Her dainty hands plucked at Azulea's sleeve. "The Market Guards are on their way."

Imperfect timing. The Elishian's gill fluttering was lessening. She didn't need outsiders escalating events again. Lowering her arm, Azulea pasted a smile on her face. "But perhaps I have been hasty? We are all friends and colleagues, correct?" She turned toward the hulking Mosa, switching back to his native tongue. "Please allow me to provide you with a gift, in thanks for the stories you will share." She turned her head in the direction of the bartender. "I know that Ribalaigua has some plum preserve hidden in a back cupboard."

She couldn't see the bartender, Ribalaigua. No doubt he was standing too far away for her to see, but he was a Costan with enough charm to fill three caravans, and his sixteen eyes saw everything that went on in the parlor. He always had some sweet liquor wrapped in one of his tentacles. "Ribalaigua? A drink for our trading friend."

"Of course, Azulea." Ribalaigua's voice was mellifluous and friendly, perfect for his role. "He has been so generous with his time, it is the least we can do." Ribalaigua's ability to defray tension with smooth words and even smoother drinks was the reason he had the job at the Residence, and especially in the Grand Parlor. "My good Mosa, I remember that it was the cerulean plum you preferred, yes?"

So many travelers from so many worlds. With so many attitudes.

Mosa didn't move. Not quite ready to give ground. Azulea touched him gently on the arm. His skin nearly burnt her fingers it was so hot. She could feel the indecision within him. "I would be appreciative if we could complete our interview, perhaps later?"

The Lacerti grunted, nodded, or at least Azulea guessed he nodded, and turned toward Ribalaigua with a bellow and growl-squeak that said the preserve had better be "the good stuff."

With one of them taken care of, Azulea turned to Davarr. She wasn't overly fond of the Elishian, and his behavior today was unbelievably provocative. Azulea frowned. No, that wasn't an accurate statement. It was aggressive.

"Don't try to work your words on me, cripple. I am not so simple," Davarr growled.

Azulea stepped right up to Davarr's chest and lifted her face to his. She'd been told that her brown eyes were still lovely, even if the centers were cloudy. She knew being direct with her unfocused gaze often made people uncomfortable. She was not afraid to use that to her advantage. They didn't know how to handle her blindness. They equally didn't know how to handle her competence.

"What is wrong, Davarr?" Azulea asked in perfect Elishian, her pitch sliding up and down over the consonants. She kept her voice soft so others didn't hear, but she didn't mince words. "You were looking for a fight." She paused, thinking. "That's not like you."

"It isn't your concern," he snapped back, biting down every word so hard she could hear his fangs click together. Scaled hands wrapped around her upper arms, not tightly. He didn't mean her harm, but he was agitated and much stronger than her.

"Please, Azulea," Peny interjected. "Can we just go? Please, can we go?"

"You there! Stop!" The words were harsh, barked out in heavily accented Trade. A split second later, Azulea flew through the air. Someone had tackled both her and Davarr to the floor. She landed with a heavy thump. The air whooshed from her lungs. Before she could regain her breath, another body fell on top of her. Her head slammed into the mat on the floor. She bit her lip. Azulea tasted blood.

"Guards, restrain him!"

The room erupted in shouting, and there was scuffling as people moved from nearby tables. A few feet away she could hear Davarr howling that he had done nothing wrong.

A hand grasped her wrist: slender fingers, strong and well calloused. They yanked her unceremoniously to her feet. "Are you all right?"

Azulea groaned inwardly. This close, with the sunlight streaming in, she could easily make out a humanoid shape with dark crimson skin and tall, lyre-shaped horns. It was Melehti, Arbiter of the Souq, leader of the Market Guard. Azulea's ex-lover.

In a world where trading was of the highest importance, it was critical that Labyrinth's gates and their attendant souq had adequate order. The Market Guards ensured murder and thievery did not become commonplace. But Melehti had taken what were a few governor-appointed security guards and turned them into an organized force that did regular patrols, checked goods for quality, and was an authority to whom traders both local and foreign could appeal if they felt slighted.

Unfortunately, Melehti had expanded her responsibilities to include the Residence, despite there being no violence in the Residence or in the Great Archive. After all, knowledge was power, and it was the Archivists who held all the knowledge of the Labyrinth. No one would dare to bring them harm. The potential loss of access was too great.

But Melehti didn't believe in that. Her people, the Mari, believed in what they could touch and taste and feel. *No knowledge in the world will protect you from a knife between the ribs.* Azulea remembered it from their many discussions and many arguments. The breakup of their relationship had been almost a year ago, but the lingering pain was still fresh.

A hand touched her face. "You're bleeding."

"I know." Azulea fought the urge to close her eyes and lean into that so familiar touch. "Please go." The words were breathless. "Melehti, I don't need you charging in—"

"What's happening here?" The voice cut through the din, and the room was instantly silent. Azulea froze. No, no, no. It was the Head Archivist, Hypatia. Her mother.

Melehti's hand dropped from Azulea's face, not quickly as if ashamed, but slowly, as if daring Azulea's mother to say something.

"Melehti and Davarr, I would see you in my office. Azulea and Peny, to your quarters. Please." Azulea winced. The "please" was present out of politeness, but it was clear that her mother was not making a request but a demand.

"And Arbiter, get your guards out of my parlor." The words were snapped out as a general would issue commands: with the expectation of immediate obedience. "This is finished."

A small, wry smile quirked the corners of Azulea's lips as

her mother echoed her own words. But it was stifled as she recalled her mother's order sending her to her room as if she were a child.

"Mother, I can speak abo—" Azulea offered.

"She's already gone," Melehti said shortly. She ordered her own guards to wait outside the entrance to the main building where the Head Archivist kept her office.

"I guess you'll be releasing me from these bindings," Davarr said smugly.

"Davarr, you shouldn't have provoked Mosa," Peny said chidingly, her words barely audible.

Davarr thrust out his chest, and his gills fluttered. "You sat with him. You spoke with him. I did not lie." The words dripped with displeasure.

Peny hunched her shoulders. "We should go." She took Azulea's arm to lead her back toward the Archive proper. Tears burned in Azulea's eyes. She wasn't going to cry. She refused to cry.

"We were there. We know how events progressed," Azulea sputtered.

"Does it matter?" Peny said. "It's been handled."

"Of course it does," Azulea snapped, then regretted it. Peny didn't deserve Azulea's rancor. "I'm sorry. I just feel like no one understands. They don't…"

"No one takes you seriously?" There was a smile in the other woman's voice. "That you aren't good enough, or capable enough?"

Azulea's anger dissipated. Peny had been hounded mercilessly by their instructors in an effort to shape her toward an impossible perfection. In addition to her superior ability to transcribe, she had the uncanny knack of engaging and befriending even the most recalcitrant merchants and traders, even when she didn't speak their language. But Peny had struggled with the dry philosophies and histories that were a mandatory part of Archivist training, and instead of support, the Academy had heaped more and more readings on her and greater punishments when she failed to live up to their standards. Until Azulea had stepped in to help her cousin.

"You are more than capable, Peny."

"That wasn't what I was alluding to. I was saying you should let it go."

Azulea stopped walking. She heard Peny take in a breath.

"I don't think I want to."

Peny released the breath in a long-suffering groan. "Azulea, no."

"I'm not a dog to be ordered around," Azulea said caustically. "I've decided. We're going to my mother's office to give our statements." With that, she let go of the other woman's arm. She turned around and strode back the way they came, her hand trailing along the wall for guidance. "It is our duty as trainees to speak and her job as Head Archivist to listen," she threw back over her shoulder, daring Peny to stop her.

Azulea knew the building by heart. She passed the hallway that led to the Grand Parlor, the noise seeping into the quiet of the main building, and kept going. She cut through the Gallery Chamber. The large room was used for feasts and dances where trading deals were made that encompassed the fortunes of whole worlds. Her steps echoed across the hardstone floor. There were no woven mats here, and she could feel the chill from the stone through the soles of her sandals. The noise reverberated around the room. From the way the sound moved, she could hear the majestic staircase to the left that curved up to the second floor.

During the New Year's celebrations, her mother would stand high above and bless the events. In many ways, the Archivists were more than just transcribers of the secrets of the Labyrinth. They were its priests and prophets, using the knowledge they gleaned from the Labyrinth for the benefit of the people.

"Azulea, wait!"

She could hear Peny clattering behind her as she struggled to catch up. The girl never could resist the latest fashions, no matter how bizarre. Her new shoes were little more than six inch wooden blades. Azulea winced as she heard Peny's steps stutter.

"You're going to fall and hurt yourself," Azulea admonished as she waited for the younger woman to catch up.

"Yes, but my shoes make my legs look incredibly long."

Azulea had no answer to that. "Come on, you can lean on me."

It wasn't like the two girls had very far to go. The Head Archivist's office was just down the private hall and the second door on the right. At the door, Azulea took a deep breath. Sometimes, having your mother as Head Archivist was overwhelmingly intimidating. You often felt that you just could never get anything right. But not this time.

Azulea heard a faint sound as she twisted the decorative handle and threw the door wide, striding in. She was ready for an argument. She stopped just inside, finally understanding what she had heard outside the door—muffled laughter.

"Azulea, knocking would be appropriate." The words came from her mother.

There was a trilled laugh to the right. Davarr.

"It's perfectly fine, Hypatia." Melehti spoke, her voice coming from the left.

Azulea's nose wrinkled as a sweet, acrid smell filled her nostrils. She coughed. The room was filled with Mu'assel smoke. The honeyed smoky mix always made her skin feel tacky and her lungs thick.

"I had heard that the Kalifas were looking for the lost

passageway to the Farnot kingdom," Davarr said, picking up the conversation from where Azulea had interrupted it.

Melehti snorted and then coughed. "Good fortune to them. They couldn't find groundworms in the feeding pits on Bashor."

Davarr laughed, a high-pitched trilling sound. "Last time I was there, it took me a week to get rid of them. They were in my clothes and my hair. All of my goods were infested."

Her mother inhaled loudly, and Azulea heard the bubbling of the argeeleh. "You are welcome to join us, if you'd like, Azulea. Though I should not reward you for such behavior."

And just like that, all words fled from Azulea's mind. In the space it had taken her to arrive at the office, her mother had already disarmed and charmed both Melehti and Davarr. Now they were all sitting around smoking sweetened Mu'assel and laughing like the incident earlier never happened.

"Peny, you might as well come in and sit too." Azulea's mother sounded like a put-upon matriarch, wearied by the antics of incompetent youth.

Azulea's anger returned. Peny slid in, wobbling, clearly nervous, and sat with a heavy oomph next to Davarr. That only left the seat on the low couch next to Melehti. Azulea sat, her posture stiff and uncomfortable. She felt similar tension from Melehti.

Melehti offered Azulea one of the many silk-covered pipes to the argeeleh bottle. Their hands touched, Melehti's bronzed skin a contrast to Azulea's own lighter olive hue.

Azulea accepted the pipe ungraciously. She stared at Melehti's hand until the other woman pulled back. Azulea put the carved mouthpiece to her lips and drew in the thick smoke. The sweet smoke slid across her tongue and rolled down her throat. Her split lip burned. She held her breath, letting the smoke swirl around her lungs before she exhaled. And with it, she felt some of her tension dissipate.

Why should she be angry? Her mother was just acting as the Head Archivist should.

"I am sorry for my behavior. It brought disorder to your house." The words came from Davarr unexpectedly. The words were awkward and stilted in Trade, but his pronunciation was easily understood.

Azulea stiffened in surprise but said nothing. She hadn't expected that. But she could also hear that his words weren't directed to her. They were to her mother. It was an apology to the Head Archivist.

"The cri...the girl did as she should." He continued, and then stopped.

Cripple to girl—an upgrade, Azulea thought acerbically. Or he was being polite in front of the Head Archivist? After all, *she* actually did have the authority to banish him.

Azulea's mother didn't speak. She drew slowly from her tube and then exhaled with equal slowness. Silence. Patience. It was a tactic Azulea had seen her use many times. She felt Melehti shift on the seat. Once, twice.

Melehti spoke, her words slow and somnolent. "I too apologize, Archivist. We acted in the interests of the Archive and to protect those in the Residence."

Azulea didn't hear anything from her mother, but from the slight movements from Melehti, she could imagine the stare her mother was likely levelling at the other woman in light of the flimsy excuse.

"But I should have asked what assistance might be rendered."

The silence continued. It lasted for one heartbeat and then another. Her mother really was that good. Azulea felt a tiny spark of pride. Archivists were usually thought of as experts in understanding words and artifacts, but in truth, the very best Archivists were as good at reading people as they were at reading texts.

Azulea's mother spoke, her voice filled with warmth and charm. "Thank you both. I am ever grateful to both of you for your contributions. You keep us informed. You keep us safe, and without you, the Archive would be poorer. Greater understanding of the Labyrinth and greater understanding of each other is what makes the Archive successful. I hope that we can continue such a fruitful relationship."

Azulea choked on the monologue from her mother. It was the highbrow language she used at feasts and in negotiations with traders. Surely, no one would believe… And yet, both Melehti and Davarr seemed to be in agreement with her.

"We will smoke on it," Davarr said, inhaling loudly.

Azulea slumped in the chair. They would now be smoking and meditating on their relationships for the next few minutes. She never had patience for this part of the ritual.

"Peny, would you get us some refreshment? Iced kahwa. We will be ready in a few minutes," the Head Archivist said.

Peny stood and clopped to the door, wobbling only once before slipping outside. Azulea heard her steps recede as she headed toward the kitchens.

"Then, until the vessel is empty," Davarr said. It was a traditional phrase used when sharing Mu'assel. That all present would remain in peace for as long as the smoke encircled them. It swirled around and in them. Shared breath, shared life. Until the vessel was empty.

Azulea had never been clear on whether the vessel was the argeeleh of Mu'assel, or the vessel was the bodies of the smokers. "Until the vessel is empty," she repeated.

Melehti was next, and finally Azulea's mother.

Five minutes later, the room was swirling with smoke so thick that Azulea imagined she could actually see it, and they were drinking the kahwa from tall glasses, the outsides beaded with condensation. Melehti finally set down her glass, and with a short bow and word of thanks, took her leave. Davarr quickly followed suit.

As the door clicked shut behind them, Azulea tensed. She knew what was coming. She stared straight ahead, not even attempting to feign sight, something she did often for the comfort of those around her.

Azulea could feel the weight of her mother's gaze. "Well…" The word trailed off to silence.

Azulea tightened her lips. She wasn't going to fall for it. She could wait her mother out. The silence stretched out between them, longer and longer.

"We were wrong. We shouldn't have done the interview in the Grand Parlor," Peny burst out.

Azulea groaned. "Peny!"

The other girl looked at her, clueless. "What?"

Azulea sighed.

"It was not only wrong, but dangerous. We don't have rules because they are nice or because they make things easy. Rules ensure that the Archive operates smoothly and safely and productively." Azulea's mother was speaking now as the Head Archivist. Her voice was firm, as if delivering a lecture to the First Year Adherents.

Azulea hated it, but her mother was right. They had been careless, but who would have thought it would devolve into a potential bar brawl?

"You don't remember, either of you, but the Residence and the Archive were not always as they are now. This was a trepidatious venture, and information was often bought not with coin, but with blood. The Labyrinth likes its secrets."

"I'm sorry, Head Archivist." Peny sounded truly contrite.

"I'm sorry, Head Archivist," Azulea echoed. "But…"

"Really, Azulea? Excuses?"

Azulea fought the urge to squirm. "No, Mother."

"Peny, you are excused." Without a word, the other woman quickly left the room, brushing a hand over Azulea's shoulder as she left.

The door closed.

"Wipe your lips. You're bleeding again." A soft cloth was pressed into her hand. She'd almost forgotten the cut on her lip.

"Azulea, you cannot keep doing this."

"Doing what?" Azulea hated the petulance in her tone, it was childish. "I am as skilled as any Archivist."

"You're leading Peny down a bad path. You cannot keep translating for her. She must learn the languages herself. Every Archivist must be wholly self-sufficient." There was a pause. "And you cannot keep using her as your eyes."

Azulea's hands curled into fists, and she could feel the skin across her knuckles strain as she clenched them. "Together we can provide all of the skills needed. Interview, transcribing, map-making, even the negotiations for payment. You know she can do it. You know I can do it. I can…"

"We've discussed this before." Her mother's words were like a lash. "We cannot risk errors or misunderstandings from having crucial knowledge pass through one individual to another before it is written. Especially not for new gates and dangerous worlds. The Labyrinth is unforgiving."

It was an old argument, one that was repeated more and more often. Especially as Peny was nearing her final years in training, and Azulea's inability to draw the maps or transcribe the information prevented her from ever testing for the role of Archivist. And yet, like the proverbial saturniid flying toward the moon, Azulea could not stop her quest. She had sacrificed friends, free time, hobbies…even Melehti.

Her grandmother, as the previous Head Archivist, had

encouraged Azulea to continue her studies and to demand a place and a role in the Archive. There had been a terrible scene, and her relationship with her mother had never quite healed. One day, possibly soon, as the day for testing drew nearer, the ongoing fight wouldn't end with her acquiescing to her mother's wishes or bending the traditions of the Archive. She wasn't looking forward to that time because after, she did not think they would ever be able to speak again.

Suddenly, the air was rent by a scream. It was Peny. Azulea's mother was out the door in a heartbeat, her robes flapping behind her. Peny screamed again. Then began shouting for help.

Azulea followed the sounds of her mother's running feet. They came from the left. She listened. Peny was in the Gallery Chamber; her voice had too much reverberation to be anywhere else.

Pulling up her robe with one hand and letting the other trace the wall, Azulea ran. She could hear shouts and the sounds of others running in the same direction. She reached the end of the hall where it opened into the Gallery Chamber and halted at the edge of that open space. She could hear the others gathered around the stairs on the far side but couldn't figure out why. And she heard a sound she had never heard before. It was her mother, sobbing.

"What is it? What's going on?" Azulea could hear the desperation and fear in her own voice.

"It's the Matriarch." Melehti took Azulea's hand and led her forward.

"Amma? What has happened to her?" Azulea asked, dazed.

"I'm so sorry. I was looking for Charemon to talk about security. I came back when I heard the screams."

Azulea followed Melehti through a growing crowd of people. She could hear whispers and crying. On the floor she could just barely make out a shadow of deep scarlet. No, it couldn't be.

Azulea went to her knees, her fingers reaching out to brush the face of the old woman who lay sprawled at the bottom of the stairs, her robes spread wide around her, a pool of red. "Grandmother?"

Tears gathered in Azulea's eyes.

"She's dead." The words came from Charemon. The old man knelt next to her, his knees creaking at the abuse. He was her grandmother's cousin and worked as the Archive's Superintendent. A large, hirsute man, his bulk pushed Azulea aside as his weathered hands reached to touch his sister but then grabbed Azulea's mother's hands. He had been a part of the Archive long before even Azulea's grandmother had risen to the role of Head Archivist. "You're distraught."

"No, no. She can't be gone!" Azulea's mother was screaming the words. She was more tormented, more hysterical, than Azulea had ever seen her.

Azulea caught herself gulping air. She let her hands trace down the old woman's face, pulling her Amma's collar closed and straightening her robe. Amma would never let herself look disheveled. She brushed grit from the red cloth and smoothed the edges gently across her grandmother's chest.

Now child, repeat it back to me. Yes, the whole scroll. Wonderful! You shall be the cleverest Archivist in all the worlds! Azulea had been six years old. It had been the first time her grandmother had espoused the idea that Azulea would be an Archivist, an idea that no one would have ever thought possible. The old woman believed in Azulea's success and from that day forward never accepted anything less than the best efforts from her granddaughter.

"Amma." The name overflowed with love. Her grandmother was the only one who understood; they shared the same ability. Both of them could remember everything they ever saw or heard or smelled or touched. It bound them tighter than even blood. And her grandmother had taught her how to use her gift in service to the Archive.

"She must have fallen down the stairs." Davarr's voice came from the growing crowd. Peny's shouts had turned to wails. They grated on Azulea's ears.

"Everyone, get back. The chirurgeon will be here shortly." Even now, Melehti was taking charge. "Charemon, will you move the body to…"

"Take her to my quarters, they're closest," Azulea's mother said, quickly coming to herself. She sniffed and cleared her throat. "Peny, be quiet."

Wiping the tears from her eyes, Azulea rose as well. A wave of dizziness hit her. She wobbled and would have fallen if Charemon hadn't caught her arm and steadied her. She swallowed reflexively as her stomach lurched. "No, I'm okay."

"You're distraught," Melehti said. It was a statement, not a question.

"Of course I'm distraught. My grandmother just died," Azulea snapped as she steadied herself on Charemon's arm. Her balance was just the slightest bit off.

"Can someone see you to your quarters?" Melehti asked, concern filling her tone.

Once again, sent to her room. "I'm fine," Azulea ground out. "Just see to my grandmother."

Someone took her hand and gently pulled her away. From the scent of persimmon and the bright gold hair, Azulea knew it was Peny. Azulea hesitated, but then followed, only stumbling once. Behind her she could hear the crowd being dispersed by Melehti and her mother instructing Charemon on carrying the body—her grandmother, Azulea corrected with a sharp ache in her heart—to the Head Archivist's own rooms. Hypatia would see to her mother herself.

"I came out and just found her there." Peny was crying and sniffling and talking all at the same time. "I've never seen anyone dead before. And she was so nice. I can't bear it." For once, Azulea didn't mind the other girl's babbling and leaned on her as they made their way back to their quarters.

"Will you be all right?" Peny asked at the door to Azulea's chambers.

Azulea offered a weak smile. "I'll be fine. Why don't you rest? I imagine all Archive work and classes for trainees will be cancelled." Not waiting for a response, she stepped into her room and gently closed the door.

She just needed a few minutes to collect herself. Azulea knew the dimensions of her room perfectly. The walls were a bare white to reflect as much light as possible throughout the room. She curled her toes into the thick carpet. The deep red was very similar to the color of Archivist robes. It was the one color that Azulea could actually "see" easily. She crossed the open space to her bed and with a heavy sigh, lay down. Her mind was awhirl with thoughts of Amma, and the tears began to flow again. She buried her face in the pillow and cried herself to sleep.

A few hours later, Azulea awoke. Her head pounded, and her mouth was dry. She felt as if she had spent a night drinking heavily. Was this grief? She sat up and reached for the water that was always by her bed. She drank greedily from it and felt better immediately.

"I need to change," she said to herself, noting that she was still in her robes from the morning. They were rumpled and untidy. She began to disrobe and stopped. They had grit on them, like fine sand. It was also on her fingers. Azulea shuddered. It was from her grandmother. She remembered brushing it off the dead woman's robes.

Her grandmother would never have gone out in public with dirt on her clothing. Azulea rubbed the dust between her fingers. It was so very fine, more a powder than dirt. She cautiously brought the cloth to her nose and sniffed it. Immediately, a faint wave of dizziness rose over her and she wobbled even though she was seated on the bed.

Vertigo? No. She sniffed again. Her stomach lurched, and she fought the urge to gag as dizziness swirled through her head and body again.

A powder that caused dizziness? What was it doing on her grandmother? Azulea frowned as she thought. Wait, she knew of this. She pulled down a book in her mind, the text rolling through her mind, word after word. It was from the Labyrinth. She'd heard about it a very long time ago when she was a little girl. It was from a world that was rarely visited. *Cinchona Aerium*.

Cold washed over Azulea and goosebumps prickled across her skin. Her Amma was an old woman, but not a frail one. She used a cane, more for show than real need, but, if someone had doused her with Cinchona, the vertigo alone would have guaranteed her fall down the stairs.

Azulea's heart skipped. It wasn't an accident. Someone had killed her Amma. Someone had killed the matriarch of the Archivists.

She had to tell someone. She had to tell her mother. As the Head Archivist, she'd know what to do. Azulea stood but just as quickly sat down again. The powder. She wriggled out of her clothing, taking care to avoid any potential leavings trapped in the fabric. Dropping her robe to the floor, she made her way over to the pitcher and basin of water on the far side of her room. Azulea picked up the small wash cloth and used it to wipe her hands vigorously.

Then she thoroughly washed her hands and face. No dizziness. Pleased at her caution, Azulea quickly pulled on fresh clothing and all but ran out the door.

One hand trailing the wall, she walked quickly through

the Archive. The smell of fresh bread and pungent meat caused her stomach to growl. It must be dinnertime. The halls were unusually quiet. Even during mealtimes, there was always one Academician or another guiding a gaggle of trainees through the building, or Chroniclers with massive tomes and papers, or even just traders on their way to and from interview suites.

The Head Archivist's quarters were not far from the Gallery Chamber, but on the third floor. Not that the Head Archivist had a specific suite. The truth was that her mother had always preferred privacy and purposely chose to live as far from her work as possible.

Azulea made her way up the back stairwell. Cool air came through the windows that opened on to the central courtyard of Archive buildings. Even through it would have been a shorter route, she couldn't bring herself to pass through the Gallery Chamber and up the very same stairs that had killed her grandmother. Her lips tightened into a thin line.

She reached the far hallway and heard voices murmuring. A door closed ahead of her, a thump of wood on stone. There was a swish of clothing and muffled steps coming toward her. Azulea squinted, wishing she could decipher who was there.

"Azulea," the voice was a contralto, raspy with grief, "it is Otha and Viera. I am so sorry."

Otha was Azulea's aunt, her mother's younger sister, and even though Azulea recognized her voice, the older woman always took care to identify herself so Azulea would never have to guess to whom she was speaking. Viera was her mother's best friend from childhood and a gifted Illuminator. To many, she was sometimes seen as cold and unfeeling, but Azulea knew that a warm nature was hidden behind the stern lines on her face.

Azulea put out her hands toward Otha. There was a

shuffle of shifting garments before her hands were clasped by the other woman. Otha's fingers were thin and dry, but with the bulbus knuckles that were telltale signs of arthritis. "How is Mother?"

"The Head Archivist bears up well," Viera said. Her voice was tight, almost mechanical. "But the bereaved daughter aches."

A second later, Azulea heard a sniffle.

"Are you crying?" Otha's voice was half surprised and half-teasing. Viera never cried. Not when her husband, a Journeyman Archivist, had beaten her so badly she couldn't walk for days nor when her six-year-old daughter had died from the Two-Year Plague.

Everyone knew Viera's story. Amma had banished Viera's husband and taken her in. She taught Viera how to decorate manuscripts, and in return, a beautiful, talented woman now supported the Archive.

There was another sniff. "No. I'm not."

Azulea let go of Otha's hands and wrapped her arms awkwardly around the tall, sparse Viera. The woman had her arms full of cloth. "I know you loved her too," Azulea whispered.

"We have to go," Viera said shortly. Her voice was thick with throttled emotion.

Azulea smiled and released her. Then her face turned solemn as she remembered her own mission. She slid between the duo and toward the door at the far end of the hall. "I will see you later. Right now, it is critical that I speak with the Head Archivist."

The pause in footsteps behind her let her know that she had aroused the women's curiosity.

Azulea knocked on the door, perhaps a little too loudly. Charemon opened it and ushered her in. There were lamps set about the room, filling the space with a brownish gloom.

"Mother?" Azulea asked, uncertain where her mother was and who else was in the room.

"I'm here," came a voice from in front of Azulea. It sounded tired.

Azulea moved toward where she knew the bed was, sliding her feet cautiously across the floor, first one, then the other. This wasn't a room she visited frequently, so she was not as sure of the dimensions. The sounds in the room were muted, perhaps tapestries on the wall? When she felt the bedcovers against her shins, she put a hand down and touched a still foot under the covers. Amma.

"I knew she was going to die someday. It is inevitable. But I thought I had more time," Azulea's mother said.

Azulea felt grief rise up, pressing against her chest. She followed the edge of the bed around to where her mother sat.

"We all think there will be more time," Charemon said from the other side of the room. "I keep thinking, 'What if…?'" His words trailed away, and he *hmm'd*, a sound low in his throat. "Your mother was an amazing woman, Hypatia," Charemon finished awkwardly.

Azulea was silent.

"Such a stupid, meaningless accident." Rage filled those words. "I should have moved her quarters to the main floor."

Azulea gulped, and grabbing her mother's arm, blurted out, "It wasn't an accident."

"What?" The word came from both Charemon and her mother.

"It wasn't an accident," Azulea repeated. "Amma was killed. She was poisoned."

The silence after Azulea's words was like a living thing, swirling between the three of them. She wondered if she was the only one holding her breath.

"Don't be ridiculous." The words came out of her mother's mouth in a burst of emotion: shock, anger…and perhaps fear?

Azulea shook her head. "No, it's true."

"You're being dramatic. This is not the time, nor place." Her mother's tone was dismissive, and she turned back to smoothing the sheets.

Charemon tried a different tack. "Azulea, you're upset." He took her arm as if to escort her from the room.

Azulea shook her arm free. She'd never realized Charemon could move so quickly and so silently. "I am upset, and you should be, too. This was murder!"

"Azulea, enough!" Her mother's words were whiplash quick. This was the Head Archivist speaking.

"No," Azulea continued doggedly. "Her clothing, it had a powder on it. I remember it. It's a powder from the Labyrinth. *Cinchona Aerium*. It causes dizziness."

"Az…"

Azulea ignored her. "I got it on my hands. That's why when I stood up I was so unsteady," she explained.

She placed a hand on her mother's shoulder. She could feel her mother's whole body trembling. "You need to listen to me!" Azulea's frustration was rising, as was her voice.

"Get out."

"What?"

"I said, get out. If you cannot respect the dead, if you cannot respect the Archive and your place in it, if you cannot respect me, then you should not be here." The words were rising in volume, thin and tight with unshed tears. "I have allowed you your fantasies over the years—to alter the traditions of the Archive—but this is too much."

"Mother, it was murder! What kind of Head Archivist allows violence under her care?"

The sound of the slap reverberated around the room. An

even louder silence followed. Azulea raised a hand to her burning cheek. Her mother had never struck her before.

One heartbeat. Two heartbeats.

"This is a terrible time for everyone." Charemon, of course. Ever the peacemaker. "Azulea, let me walk you out."

Azulea opened her mouth to object. She couldn't let this happen. There was too much at stake. She had to stay and make them listen.

"This is not a good time," he added quickly, pulling her away from the bed.

"I just need Amma's clothes." She called out over her shoulder, "We can have it tested. Garoq can test it. We can prove it wasn't an accident!"

"Garoq?!" Charemon spit the word out. His hands were like a vice on her arm; slowly, interminably, she was being pulled to the door. "The boy is a fledgling, foolish, and imprudent."

Azulea heard a soft sob. "Please just go, Azulea. Your wild ideas don't make a difference. No one saw any powder, or a poisoner, and the clothing has already gone to be burned. Otha and Viera took it."

"No," Azulea murmured as Charemon dragged her into the hall. He closed the door behind them. She had missed her chance. Her aunts had had the clothing in their arms, and she hadn't seen it. She couldn't have seen it. And now she was too late. All the fight left her.

As if sensing it, Charemon let go of her arm. "I'm sorry, Azulea. Truly." He *hmm'd*, the sound thick between them, and then grunted as if making a decision. "Are you sure?"

Azulea froze. "Yes. No. Maybe. But I will find out," she declared. Steel edged her tone.

The big man *hmm'd* again. It was an old habit, a vocal tic. "I don't know. It isn't my place to say, but there have been rumors and discontented mutters."

"What are you talking about?" Azulea was impatient, unsure how this connected to her grandmother.

He drew in a long breath. "I don't know details, but I do know your Amma banished several traders years ago. Traders that your mother reinstated recently."

"Why would my mother do that?" Azulea asked. "The Residence is a sanctuary. I didn't even know banishments could be lifted."

"Yes, but these traders carried information from the fringe worlds. Whole caravans sworn by blood and bile to never speak to the Archive. It is knowledge we could never receive any other way."

Realization hit. "Like the Lacerti, Mosa."

Charemon *hmm'd* in agreement. "He is one who was previously banished. Your mother thought it critical for the Archive to know of these lost worlds."

"So you think it might have been one of them who killed Amma?" Azulea asked.

Charemon paused. "I believe in evidence. Your word, trainee, means little. Without proof, there is nothing but a beloved grandmother's fall."

Azulea touched a hand to her cheek. The memory of her mother's slap was still a vivid warmth under her fingertips. She then touched the wood of the closed door. She wasn't sure if she imagined it or not, but she thought she could hear crying behind it. "But I can't just ignore it."

"No, I didn't think you would," Charemon said.

He sounded distracted, as if his thoughts were elsewhere.

"Thank you, Charemon," Azulea said with fervor.

She headed back down the hall, her steps suddenly speeding up. An idea had just occurred to her. Perhaps she did have something for Garoq after all. Behind her, she heard the Head Archivist's door open and then close.

Once back in her room, Azulea pulled the washcloth from beside her basin and scooped up her clothing off the floor, being careful not to bring it close to her face. She wrapped it into a tight ball and shoved it into a cloth bag. Hefting her burden, she picked up her long cane and headed out.

The Academy was one of the buildings on the far side of the square behind the Main building and the Residence, where the traders stayed. The Academy was where the great philosophers and teachers from a multitude of worlds taught. The Archive was more than just a repository of knowledge. It was a part of a vast network of buildings, an institute of great learning.

The Archive Repository, with its collection of artifacts, books, parchments, and manuscripts was a series of tall stone buildings that flanked the square. The buildings were connected on the ground by well-worn paths and on the upper stories by soaring arches of stone. It made Azulea's heart swell with pride. Her ancestors had conceived of this; they had built this.

Stepping out the door into the open square, she grimaced. Her feet hit the hardened pitch paving the pathways between the buildings. She hated going out-of-doors on her own with just her cane. There was so much open space. It was easy to get disoriented, and Azulea hated being seen as less than capable. Sweeping it left then right, the cane let her feel the path in front of her, leading from the Archive to the Academy.

Thankfully, this time of evening, the buildings were less busy as classes were finished for the day. Other than the few nocturnal traders, it was rare for interviews to be conducted this late. In fact, many of the people employed by the Archive had already returned home for the day. Azulea turned her face skyward, feeling the rays of sunlight weakening as night fell. However, she knew Garoq, and she had no doubt that he would still be hard at work on his multitude of projects. When not teaching, he was constantly researching and experimenting with ways to break down and reassemble different materials—wood, metal, cloth. In other worlds, he would have been called an alchemist. Her lips quirked. Although she'd never seen him turn lead into gold, she had seen him turn a skein of silk into a smoking, flaming inferno.

"Garoq?" Azulea entered the laboratory after her knock yielded no response. She could barely make out a faint lightening of the darkness in a far corner of the large room. Azulea headed toward it. She stopped as she slammed her hip into a heavy wooden table. She let out a cry of pain and then hissed a few choice curse words. She rubbed the area. It was definitely going to bruise. She proceeded more cautiously. "Garoq?"

"Back here," a reedy voice answered.

Finally.

Azulea slowly moved toward the faint, bright spot in her vision.

"Who is there?"

"Azulea," she answered, coming level with a table that felt like it had several candles on it. The heat radiating from the surface forced her to lean back.

"Careful, there's a boiling alembic there as well as the candles."

"Not quite boiling yet," she said. "I don't hear the bubbles coming to the surface, but close. What are you doing?"

He chuckled, and Azulea was immediately on her guard. She and Garoq had been classmates during her early training. She remembered him as being a stout young Escuilliei with an intense presence, a wide beak, and a quick laugh. His bright green feathered form and vanilla scent made him immediately identifiable. She also remembered him as an inveterate prankster.

"Sit here," Garoq said, shoving a seat under her. Azulea fell, as gracefully as she could, into the chair.

"Uh, thank you."

Garoq pressed a small glass into her palm. It sloshed over her hand in his excitement.

"What?"

"Taste it."

"What?" Her instincts were screaming at her not to.

"Go on. Taste it!"

"I swear, Garoq if this is a joke." Azulea turned toward the place where she imagined he stood.

"No joke."

She wasn't convinced. "Is it safe?"

"Of course not," he snorted and then cackled with glee.

Azulea brought it up to her nose.

"No, no." She felt his hand pushing the glass down, away from her nose.

"Just taste."

She gave him a skeptical look before lifting the glass to her lips and swallowing the small dram of liquid.

Suddenly her mouth was on fire. Then her throat. Then her stomach. It burned the whole way down. Azulea coughed and gasped for breath, tears coming to her eyes. "Oh my garden and hearth gods!" She couldn't even think.

Garoq's chortles were thin quacks of sound. "Well?" he asked, impatient for her response.

Azulea wiped her eyes on her sleeve and coughed once more. She sniffed the glass. No wonder he had stopped her.

"You're making alcohol?!" she gasped, her voice a little raspy.

"I know it's a bit rough, but I think I'm close."

"Close to what?" Azulea wasn't sure she wanted to know the answer.

"I am perfecting the recipe. An exact copy of the liquor from Thujone, but without those pesky worms that devour your intestines."

Azulea groaned. "I don't know if my intestines are still in their original condition after that."

"Good. Then it's working."

"Ugh." Azulea set the glass down, careful of the candles and dripping wax on the table. "Garoq, I have a favor to ask."

Garoq was, at once, all seriousness. "Of course. What do you need?"

Azulea paused. "How much of this stuff have you drank?"

"None. You were the first."

She could practically hear his smugness.

"I'm honored." Azulea's voice was heavy with sarcasm.

"I knew you'd feel that way." Garoq's humor came through. There was a pause, and then he was serious, all humor gone. "I thought you could use a drink. I heard about your grandmother. I'm very sorry."

"This is about that." Azulea took a breath. Dare she tell Garoq? Would he respond the way her mother had? "You cannot tell anyone. Please."

"Very mysterious."

Azulea didn't answer.

"Really?"

"Swear to me."

"All right. I promise."

Azulea weighed her thoughts. She knew Garoq. It didn't matter what he said; the Escuilliei couldn't keep a secret. He was the biggest gossip. No, it didn't matter. This was too important.

"Grandmother was poisoned."

"What?" The shock in his voice couldn't be faked. "But how?"

Azulea pushed the bag of clothing into his hands. "I suspect it was *Cinchona Aerium.*"

"*Cinchona Aerium?*" he repeated as if not quite understanding.

"From the Green Sky world," Azulea continued. "This powder was on her clothing. I think they hoped to hide it, to let us think it was an accident."

"Azulea…" Garoq started.

Azulea held up a hand. "Stop. I've already heard all of the ways this idea is preposterous. That is why I need you. I need you to test the clothing. Prove that it was murder."

"Or not," he said, his voice barely audible.

"Or not." Azulea nodded. "Either way, I must know. I believe she was killed. I can feel it, but I need proof."

"*Cinchona Aerium…* No one has been to Green Sky world in a long time," Garoq said thoughtfully, "or collected any of the pollen for *Cinchona.*" He pulled the clothing out of the bag, careful to preserve any potential powder. "Still, I think I can find a way to test for it."

"You'll do it? Thank you. You have no idea how much this means." Azulea felt the words pouring from her. No response. Garoq had already turned to a nearby table and begun examining the cloth, muttering to himself, "Faint staining. A few grains."

"Where would they have gotten it?" Azulea asked.

Garoq shrugged, the slight sound of his feathers rustling complementing the sound of the bubbling still. "I am not sure, but I may have your answer about what this is in a day or two."

Azulea nodded. "Thank you. And please…"

"I know. Don't tell anyone."

It was the Vigil Night. Azulea knew her mother would sit with Amma until the morning, along with Charemon and the aunts. Only family one step away could keep vigil with the body. Those who knew her best would sit the last watch to ensure her soul was truly gone. They would sit and sing and tell stories about her, sharing memories. Memories that would prove to any recalcitrant spirit they would not be forgotten so that they could move on to their next life.

But those were not the thoughts swirling through Azulea's head on the walk back to her room. Who would want to kill her grandmother? Charemon had mentioned problems with some of the Traders, but that didn't make sense. If they had just been allowed to return, why would they jeopardize that? They had accepted her mother's lifting of the banishment, so they must have seen some value to accessing the Archive's resources.

Azulea grunted and let out an epithet as her cane caught in the uneven ground, causing her to stumble and jabbing her in the stomach. She shook her head, disgusted at her own distractedness.

"Terrible language for a beautiful lady. From your grace and poise, I know it is the dirt here in the Shining City that did you wrong. I would swear that it leaps up and grabs one's ankles. Are you all right?"

Azulea squinted, but it was past dark now, and she could see nothing. She pasted a self-deprecating smile on her face, but her voice was stiff. "I am fine." She hid her embarrassment poorly.

"Don't be so defensive, Zuzu."

Recognition hit her, and Azulea scowled. "Don't call me that." She kept walking, doing her best to ignore the tall figure with a rolling gait that stepped up to her side. Handsome Dan was a regular at the Residence, a guide and caravan captain of some skill who changed employers and merchant masters the way Azulea changed clothing.

"I'm sorry," he said, with a half-chuckle that belied his words. "But it is fun to make you angry."

The explanation did not make it any better. "This is not the time," Azulea snapped, picking up her pace, the cane whipping back and forth across the ground with a violence that matched her mood.

She felt a hand on her arm, firm and warm, pulling her to a halt. She felt goosebumps rise on her skin. Why did everyone feel like they had to grab her or touch her when talking to her?

"You're right. Now is not the time. I heard about your grandmother. I will share my memories tomorrow. She was a wonderful, if stern, woman."

Handsome Dan let go of her arm, and she could tell he was rubbing his knuckles. "She was quick with her cane in the classroom."

Azulea felt tears well at the memory. "Only if you were being foolish."

Handsome Dan laughed. "She was quick with her cane out of the classroom, too."

"I repeat, only if you were being foolish."

"Are you calling me a fool?"

Azulea wiped her eyes on her sleeve and offered a smile. "I would not dare disagree with my grandmother."

"That's the Azulea I know. Fierce." He touched her cheek. From anyone else, it could have been seen as a romantic gesture. Azulea knew better. From Handsome Dan, it was how he related to the world.

Azulea started walking again. The wind was picking up, and she could smell rain in the air. Handsome Dan stayed beside her, the odd clump-thump of his one-legged gait soothing. She slowed her pace so he could more easily keep up.

"You can stop the pretense with me. I know that you were intimate with my grandmother." Azulea struggled over the sentence.

Handsome Dan's voice carried a melodious lilt, even when speaking Trade. "I was. And I shall miss her terribly."

Amma had been very discreet about her personal life, but Azulea had caught Handsome Dan literally climbing out of her grandmother's window a few years earlier. Despite a marked difference in ages, Handsome Dan's promiscuous ways, and the fact that Amma openly disapproved of his reckless behavior and ridiculous fabrications, Azulea had known there was a true connection between her grandmother and the caravan captain.

Perhaps she should take Dan into her confidence. After all, she knew he cared about her Amma. Wouldn't he believe her and want to discover the murderer? Azulea's thoughts froze. Unless he had a hand in her grandmother's death.

"Were you there?" Azulea asked, feigning casualness. "When it happened?"

Dan grunted as the tentacled symbiote that acted as his missing leg slipped on the grass and he caught himself with a jerk. "No. I was…elsewhere."

Azulea frowned. "Where?"

"In the Grand Chamber. I was trying to broker a deal for a caravan to Torani." He paused. "Your grandmother and I, we had said our goodbyes."

"You threw her over?" Azulea's voice rose. "For another conquest?"

"Hell and hearthfire, no!" Dan raised his hands. "She quit me. I swear."

"I guess I shouldn't be surprised," Azulea responded, the heat sliding out of her.

"Probably not." The smile was back.

They walked in silence for a few minutes. Dan spoke. "You don't have to stay here."

They had reached the door to the main building, and Azulea breathed a sigh of relief. She hoped that would end the conversation and she could leave Dan to whatever little game he was playing. She also didn't want to have the conversation she knew was coming again. Dan *always* brought up the same request. He'd been doing it for years, ignoring her ongoing refusals.

"I want to be an Archivist," Azulea said. She practically growled the words.

"I know, I know," Dan soothed. "Trust me, your grandmother was pretty firm on that point. She believed you would do well here."

"You talked about me?" Azulea stepped into the Residence. The temperature difference between inside and outside was muted in the evening, but during the day, the Archive's buildings remained cool.

Handsome Dan followed doggedly. "Of course." He stopped and touched her again, as if letting her know that he was still there. "It's just, I want you to know there's always an alternative. You would do well here," he repeated. "She wasn't wrong. But Azulea, I think you could do so much more."

He paused. "I loved your grandmother. As much as I can love anyone, and Azulea, you're like her. Smart and funny and unafraid. If they refuse you a place as an Archivist, then I hope you'll reconsider joining my caravan."

Azulea shook her head. "I cannot see…"

"The Labyrinth doesn't care about whether you can see or not." The words came out of Handsome Dan quickly, as if he had been holding them for a long time. "You know the pathways to travel. You have an entire Archive in your head.

Taste, smell, touch... There are so many worlds out there, and you could experience them."

"Your grandmother knew that. She didn't object to my asking you," he added. "I think, sometimes, she might have hoped—"

"No." Azulea's answer was short and sharp.

"I know." The words came from him flat and deflated. "But I'll ask again. And again. And maybe one day, you will say yes."

"Dan..."

He didn't stop. "In the interim, there is a beautiful Minoan waiting for me in my room, and a bottle of sweet preserve brandy."

Azulea rubbed her brow. The bartender would not be happy to discover his favorite secret stash had been raided.

"How did you...never mind. Goodnight, Dan."

"Goodnight, Azulea. May your memories keep you warm."

And with that, Handsome Dan disappeared further into the building, his uneven steps fading away. Azulea turned right to the back staircase that would lead her toward her personal quarters.

She was tired and heartsick, and there was so much she just didn't understand. But tomorrow, tomorrow she would begin her investigation in earnest.

※

Azulea woke to pounding on her door. She sat up blearily. She could not feel the warmth of the sun coming into her room, and the dull gray shadows intimated that dawn was only beginning. She rubbed her eyes and stretched.

"Azulea, wake up!"

It was Peny.

"I'm coming. I'm coming." For a split second, she couldn't think of why Peny would be here so early, and then it hit her, like a punch to the chest. Amma. The fall. Her death. The powder.

Azulea bit back her grief. She didn't want to grieve. Not yet. Not until she found who had killed her grandmother.

Sliding out of her bed, she crossed the room and cracked open the door. Peny pushed past her. "You aren't even dressed!"

Azulea could hear the woman pulling clothing from her wardrobe on the far side of the room.

"You must get ready for the Sharing." Peny was a whirlwind of motion.

Azulea rubbed her temples and tried not to groan aloud. She poured the last of the water from her pitcher to her basin and made her morning ablutions. Remembering too late that she hadn't replaced the towel she'd given to Garoq, she horrified Peny by drying herself with her nightclothes.

She could smell that the kitchens had been busy. The scent of warm bread wafted in her open window, and outside the street and market noises were signaling the start of the day.

"It is very early yet," Azulea commented.

"Yes, but the mourners are already gathering. The line of those here to see your grandmother stretches halfway across the souq," Peny said, placing clothing in Azulea's hands.

Azulea ran her fingers over the heavy beading. Her formal robes. She touched the embroidery on the headscarf. Her grandmother had helped her with the pattern. She swallowed and then swallowed again. She pushed her feelings down and turned an arched eyebrow at Peny.

"You know, I am perfectly capable of doing this myself."

"Yes, but you're also not capable of getting anywhere on

time," Peny huffed back. "I do not want the Head Archivist angry with me."

At that, Azulea's had snapped up. "My mother sent you?"

Peny paused. "No. Charemon asked that I make sure you were present before any others were allowed in."

"Oh." A weight settled on Azulea. Her lips formed a thin line, and she ran a brush quickly through her hair before following Peny out the door.

Azulea sat with a smile on her face. She nodded, listening to a merchant from the nearby world of Cassia talk about a visit her grandmother had had with the head of his noble house and the glory that would surely shine down upon her for her true and fair dealings.

Azulea heard him spit in his palm. With his other hand, he grabbed her wrist, the multi-segmented fingers wrapping around it twice and pressed her palm against his, the warm liquid squelching stickily between.

"Thank you," she said softly. In a desert world, to share liquid was precious. "It is a loss to our family." She turned in the direction of her mother. "But the Archive continues. Knowledge has come before, and knowledge will continue to come. And we will share with all the worlds."

The words were formal, traditional, and they tasted like dust in her mouth. She couldn't remember how many times she had already said them today, how many stories she had heard about her grandmother. How she had captured a Flavian ring-tailed lemur that the children of a merchant had smuggled into the Archive. They hadn't known that it secreted oils that curled the pages of the books nor that it produced a noxious gas that prevented all but the most hardy of travelers (or those with the strongest stomachs) from staying in the Residence for over a week. How she had barricaded the Archive when the great rebellion had happened more than forty years ago, and there had been rioting and looting in the streets. How, under her reign, the Archive had provided the cure to a pandemic in one world and helped to restore an endangered animal in another.

It was now well past noon, and the number of visitors had slowed. While her mother and other family members wove through the crowds in the Dayroom, Azulea sat on a thick rug on the east side of the room. She hated feeling like an invalid, waiting for people to come to her. And of course, in all of this, her mother refused to speak to her. In fact, she hadn't acknowledged Azulea all morning.

Azulea stood and stretched as discreetly as she could. Her legs and back ached. "You should take a break." The words startled her, and she jumped. It was her aunt, Otha. "You look tired."

Azulea felt her anger flare. She was perfectly able to sit all day and talk to people. "But…"

"Give your cousins a chance to sit vigil and share. It isn't a big room, you know. Many are still waiting for their opportunity."

Azulea ducked her head and blushed, ashamed at where her thoughts had gone.

"But my mother…"

"Is the Head Archivist, and it is Hypatia's duty to be here," Otha interrupted. There was a pause. "And I already had Viera and Charemon escort her out for at least an hour's rest."

Her aunts could be quite formidable. Azulea held up her hands in resignation. "I'll go. I'll go. Maybe I'll check in the kitchen and see if any assistance is needed."

There was a snort. From the direction, Azulea could guess that her aunt was scanning the room. "Many guests have brought tokens of their esteem. We will not run out of food. Truly, there is enough to last for the next six months. Go rest."

"Thank you, Auntie."

As if sensing something in her words, Otha wrapped her arms around Azulea. Azulea heard a small sob. "We all will miss her."

Sensing an opportunity, Azulea spoke. "But not everyone, right? Weren't there traders who were banned from the Archive?"

Otha pulled away. "Who told you that?" Her words were a whisper.

"I'm sorry. It is a secret?"

Otha cleared her throat. "No. Not a secret. But what made you think to speak of that now?" Her words were thoughtful, prying.

Azulea shook her head. "Just so many stories I've heard today and so many people…" The disambiguation came easily to her.

"I suppose so," her aunt said, as if dismissing the entire conversation, "but that was many years ago, and they have all returned—Mosa, Higu, Maser Ali, the High Pavilion Trade Consortium. Mostly far outworlders. Several are even here today."

"Really?" Azulea perked up. "Who?"

Her aunt didn't answer.

"I met Mosa the other day," Azulea offered, sensing her aunt was getting suspicious.

"Yes, we all heard about that," her aunt said acerbically.

Azulea cursed inwardly.

"You should know better than that."

Azulea wasn't going to hear any more information that might be useful. Instead, she was going to get a lecture.

"I should go take that rest," she said, when Otha paused

for breath. Azulea fairly dashed from the room, trying not to bump any of the guests. She would get something to eat from the kitchens. Afterward, she would make plans for how to proceed. After being forced to sit for most of the day and talk about her grandmother, Azulea was impatient to get back to her goal: to find out who had killed her grandmother.

Murder. The most heinous act one individual can perpetrate on another. It is taking away not only their essence but destroying all of the choices and opportunities and changes that individual would make on the universe in the times to come. It obliterated them from all the worlds for all time. Azulea shuddered, recalling the words from a philosophy lecture she'd attended as a teen.

She nibbled at her aish. The bread was still warm. Inside, the tiny chopped-up pieces of tarandro liver fried with garlic pearls, curly peppers, chili greens, and cumin teased her palate. Even with such dark thoughts, she found that she ate every bite.

Azulea closed her eyes and leaned back against the warm stone of the main building, letting her mind carry her. Her grandmother had taught her to let her thoughts flow where they would and to follow them. She would find the recollection she was looking for, but forcing it would never work.

Murder, murderers, killing, motivations. There were not so many reasons that people would be desperate enough to kill.

People killed for several things: anger, greed, revenge, passion. Who benefited from her death? Did someone disagree with her values? But why would her values matter? She had not been Head Archivist for these last ten years.

None of the reasons fit. She needed a clue. Some avenue to continue her investigation while she waited on Garoq.

Opening her eyes, Azulea sat up. She could talk to Melehti. In addition to being the Arbiter and head of the Market Guard, she was also one of the smartest women Azulea knew. If anyone could help with the investigation, she could.

She took a deep breath. She inhaled slowly and the exhaled equally slowly. This wouldn't be easy. The Archive never shared its problems with the outside world. But the bigger problem were the unresolved feelings between her and Melehti. It was complicated. There was no single word that explained the roiling in her stomach. And she was pretty sure it wasn't her lunch. Could she go to Melehti and ask for help? Seeing her yesterday was…

Azulea lifted her chin. They had parted ways. The relationship was over. This was a request from one professional to another. Yes. That made sense. She could do that. Azulea brushed crumbs from her robes. After a quick detour to her room to fetch her cane, she set out into the heart of the souq.

The souq in the Shining City was a huge affair with actual paved streets and permanent stalls as well as the temporary tents and minor markets that tended to bloom when business was booming. Banners flapped above from the buildings and all around was a riot of color and scent and sound. Azulea stuck to the paved roads she knew, letting her senses guide her.

Tamir's shawarma stand, Ariane and her spice stall, Barseyd the weaver with his giant loom, clicking and clacking. All around her, her senses were buffeted by the noise and smells of so many people. Many brushed past her, but no one bumped into her. Sometimes, being blind among the masses didn't make you invisible, it made you stand out. Most who did not know her cleared the way in front of her cane and unfocused gaze. Of course, that wasn't everyone.

"Azulea! You must come! Taste my new spice blend."

She smiled toward Ariane and waved but didn't stop moving.

"Flowers. Beautiful flowers from the lands beyond the great azure gate. Their scent alone will intoxicate you."

"Azulea, we have a new nut bread. Perfect for the Archive. Helps with mental focus."

"Lady, hey lady! A tonic. I have many tonics. To soothe your bones and clear your sight." Azulea didn't even acknowledge that call. She'd heard enough charlatans. All her life, she had lived with people talking about what she was missing instead of what she had.

A hand caught hers, and she froze. "Azulea, my sympathies to you and your family. The loss of the Mistress of the House of Books is great indeed." She relaxed. It was Halassie, one of the merchants of the bazaar. "I could not come to the Sharing, but…" He pressed a small fruit into her hand. "For your mother."

Azulea put it to her nose. It was sweet and musty, a faint fuzz all over the fruit's skin. An orchid fruit, and far out of season. "Thank you, Halassie. Your kindness is welcome." She leaned up and kissed him gently on each cheek. He returned the gesture before disappearing back to his stall.

Her destination was a low stone building near the center of the souq. Although it was the central outpost for the City Guard, it was little more than a block with a couple of rooms inside. They had actual barracks and outposts at several points in the Shining City, but this one was closest to the souq. She stopped across the street, trying to decide if she truly wanted to continue.

A line of Uthwamy women passed in front. They were walking back to their houses of hair outside the city, chatting brightly with each other. With braided quoits on their head that balanced great urns of water, they moved with grace, efficiency, and a flirtatious eye.

Perhaps it was a sign. Azulea took a deep breath and crossed the street to the front of the building.

"How may I assist you, lady?" The accent was thick and the words mumbled, as if the speaker had taken too many blows to the face.

Azulea offered her best smile. "I'm looking for Melehti."

"*Arbiter* Melehti," he repeated, stressing the honorific, "is considering a contract dispute and cannot be disturbed."

"It's all right, Zareb," came a voice from inside. "I'll see her."

The guard's body was stiff as he snapped out a quick, "Yes, Arbiter."

"Your Arbiter has good ears," Azulea offered.

"My Arbiter listens well," Zareb replied stonily. "This way, lady." He turned and disappeared inside. His steps were slow and ponderous, and Azulea could feel the air displacement as he moved. He was a large man, a very large man.

Azulea cleared her throat. She didn't want to, but she would need a guide. The inside of the building was so dark that it was impossible for her to see anything at all. Azulea was loath to attempt to navigate it on her own, even with her cane. She waited.

The guard returned. He took her arm and led Azulea into the darkness. He took her down the hall and then took an abrupt right into a small room. Faint light from tiny windows above filtered down, but the room was still too dark for Azulea's vision.

"Thank you, Zareb," Melehti said. "Close the door behind you."

The large man moved smoothly, and the wooden door closed behind him with only the faintest swish of air.

"There is a chair in front of you to the left." Melehti's words were casual, is if giving directions to someone on the street. It instantly put Azulea at ease.

She found the chair with her free hand and sat.

Silence.

Melehti leaned back in her chair, the wood creaking and groaning. "The Sharing is today, and yet, you are here. I know you, Azulea. What is it you want?"

Azulea felt the tension coil in her stomach. "I need your help."

The chair creaked again, this time as Meleta sat forward sharply.

Azulea continued. "I need to know who was in the Gallery Chamber when my grandmother was killed."

The air hissed between Melehti's teeth as the import of what Azulea was saying hit her.

"Yes, she was murdered," Azulea said firmly. "And I'll be able to prove it soon, but I need to know who was there. It had to be someone close to her. Either they ran away…"

"Or they stayed to be sure the fall killed her," Melehti finished.

"So, you believe me?"

"Why wouldn't I believe you?" Melehti retorted. The chair creaked again as Melehti leaned even further forward. With her face so close, Azulea could feel the warmth of her breath. "This was always our problem. You just couldn't trust…"

"Well, I'm here now," Azulea interrupted. "Are you going to help me or not?"

When Melehti didn't answer immediately, Azulea shot to her feet, fighting the urge to cry.

Instantly, Melehti was around the table and in front of her, and the next thing Azulea knew, she felt soft lips on her own. A second later, Azulea realized she was kissing the other woman back. Melehti's scent filled her senses, earthy and dark, like *elakkai* fruit but with a playful hint of something floral. Her fingers reached up to twine around one of Melehti's horns, and her head swam with memories unbidden—the two of them, together. *Azulea, I want to always see you like this, clothed in nothing more than sweat and moonlight.* Her breath quickened as she was drawn further into the recollection. An arm snaked around Azulea's waist, and the kiss grew firmer and more demanding. *We argue, then we make love, but we will give to and take from each other. Today, tomorrow, and all the sunrises and sunsets that follow. Azulea, I promise you this.* But Azulea had walked away.

Azulea turned her head, breaking the kiss. "I'm sorry."

Melehti's voice was barely a whisper. "I am not." She released Azulea and stepped away.

"But I will respect your decision." Melehti was all business now. *No matter how wrong I think you are.* The words were unspoken but still hung in the air between them.

Melehti rounded the desk and sat back down as if the physical space between them would resolve the tension. "Where would you like to begin this investigation?"

Azulea tried to slow the hammering of her heart. She put a hand on the chair back to both orient and steady herself. After the kiss, she wasn't sure what she needed more. Their relationship had flared white hot, and its dissolution had been just as impassioned. It had only been a year, but she had truly missed Melehti. She closed her eyes and took a deep breath and then another. She forced the remembrances away, pulling herself forcefully, violently, back to the present.

Azulea sat, landing heavily in the chair, which groaned in protest. "I was thinking we could start with a list of suspects."

"Good. Who was there, at that time, at that location? Who would have the best opportunity to push her?" Melehti said. She cycled quickly from question to question.

Azulea shook her head. "She wasn't pushed. She was poisoned."

"Poisoned?" Melehti echoed.

Azulea nodded. "I'm pretty sure it was *Cinchona Aerium*."

"I don't know that poison," Melehti said.

"It came from the Labyrinth. I don't think many people would know of it." Azulea paused. "Charemon mentioned trouble with traders?"

"There have been problems in the last few months," Melehti added thoughtfully. "Some unrest, nothing substantial though."

"He'd mentioned that Amma had banned some traders before? Ones who had brought back dangerous items. And my mother was allowing their return, giving them access to the Archive. But what does that have to do with the souq? Have there been problems requiring the Market Guard's intervention?"

Melehti's fingers tapped impatiently on the desktop. "Anytime you add a new world on a route or bring in something new, it takes time for the market to get familiar with the product, for other traders and buyers to understand the value and prices, and in truth, to see how it shifts the money and power amongst the merchants. That has been the case for the last few months. A few insults, a drunken fight or two, complaints about favoritism and tipped scales."

"And now everyone wants access to those same treasures," Azulea said, understanding. "And considering the poison was from Green Sky world, not many would have access." She stopped. "But that doesn't explain why they would murder an old woman. That puts their access to the Archive at risk again."

"It doesn't make sense. But murder doesn't have to make sense." Melehti's fingers tapped faster, as if they were trying to keep pace with her thoughts. "It isn't about knowledge and logic and patterns. It is about emotion and passion. Revenge would be a very good reason to kill your grandmother."

"So we are back to who had the opportunity," Azulea replied.

"And who was there," Melehti said in agreement. "Tell me what you know."

Azulea started ticking them off on her fingers: "Me, my mother, Peny, Charemon, you…" Azulea frowned. "The other voices were all murmurs in the crowd. I don't think I could identify them. Maybe Davarr."

"Do you think it was one of them?" Melehti asked.

"That is my family."

"And most murders are committed by family members."

Azulea shook her head. "I don't want to think so."

"There were a few more people present," Melehti said. The tapping slowed, then ceased. Azulea heard the rustle of paper as the other woman wrote her thoughts down as she spoke. "Many came in later. At least initially: you, your mother, Charemon, Peny, me, Davarr, Mosa, Kyrtos, two Pyloreans came from the back hallways with a couple of Archivists, a blue woman with tentacles for hair."

"Don't be racist," Azulea admonished.

"I'm not," Melehti grumbled. "It was a description. A woman Archivist," she repeated, "and a bearded man, also dressed as an Archivist. He was…" she said, as if searching for a word, "…rotund."

Azulea swallowed a laugh.

"And wore a three-ringed belt," Melehti finished.

"Journeyman Miles, I think," Azulea said.

"That's it. Everyone else came some few minutes later."

Azulea sat back. It didn't sound promising. She knew most of them and couldn't imagine any of them having cause to kill her grandmother.

"And that miscreant caravan captain, Danislav. He came from upstairs," Melehti added in disgust. "I'd know that tentacle symbiote limp anywhere."

Azulea was aware of the ongoing conflict between the two. Melehti was not a fan of the caravan captain. She had called Handsome Dan imperious, reckless, and high-handed. The men from his caravan had ended up in her Overnight Holding on many occasions and been charged fines for damage to taverns and stalls in the souq from rowdy drunken celebrations. He thought Melehti an uptight bitch.

"Handsome Dan," Azulea breathed.

"I certainly wouldn't call him handsome," Melehti countered peevishly. "Is that helpful?"

"Yes. Very helpful," Azulea said. Handsome Dan had lied to her. She stood, pulling on her outer robe and headscarf.

"Are you going to tell me anymore?" Melehti's voice was sharp. "Or am I to be used and left behind again?"

"Yes. I mean, no. I mean, just give me a little time," Azulea stuttered.

"You came to me," Melehti pointed out. "You ask for my help, tell me there has been a murder, and then walk away?" Her words were bitter.

"It's Archive business," Azulea said, grasping for words to explain. "I have already spoken out of turn just getting you involved."

"No."

Azulea felt as if the blood in her veins was churning throughout her body. "You're going to tell the Governor about the powder? But this is Archive business."

Melehti's voice was grim. "The Archive is too important to the Shining City. Disruption there leads to disruption here, in the city. A few drunken brawls are one issue, but the murder of the matriarch of the Great Archive is a whole different matter. I will handle this."

Tears glossed in Azulea's eyes, but she wouldn't shed them. Melehti didn't deserve them.

"It's my job, Azulea."

"No. It's what you want to do. You want to investigate this. You want to be inside the Archive. You're telling me to run along and let the adults manage the problem. You always had to tell me what to do. You had to take care of me. Like everyone else. That was the problem a year ago, and that's the problem now." Azulea felt like every word burned as it left her mouth. "I trusted you with this, now I just need a little time. Let me try to solve it myself." The last words were a plea. Azulea hated the desperation that laced them.

"Clean your house, Azulea, before we do it for you. You have three days." Melehti's words were sharp and painful, like broken glass.

Azulea walked out, trying hard to keep her head high. She didn't remember the walk back through the souq or the walk through the Archive's main building to her room. There she collapsed on the bed and cried as if her heart was breaking all over again.

⁂

The day quickly passed to afternoon, and Azulea joined the rest of her family as they wrapped Amma in her burial clothes. They laid her on a large white sheet. The cloth was thick and heavy and yellowed with age. Every family member grasped the edge and carried her together. The loss was a shared burden. They walked to the city of the dead in a silence that grew heavier each minute. Azulea wondered how the pain in her heart weighed more than the frail remains of the woman they carried.

Behind her, Azulea could hear the creaks and groans of a heavy wagon as it made its way over the uneven ground. It carried those too young or too infirm to make the two-hour walk there. She had already waved away too-helpful cousins who had asked if she would prefer to ride. Azulea clutched the sheet tightly in her right hand, cane in her left, and tried not to cry. In front of her, Peny wept loudly. Azulea tucked the cane under her arm and rested her hand against Peny's back, rubbing occasionally in slow, soothing circles. Peny only sobbed louder.

Per tradition, Amma would be buried before the sun set: a symbol of the darkness that came with the loss of an elder. They dug the hole together, each taking a turn with pick and shovel. Amma's body was lowered in, and then the grave was closed, one handful of dirt at a time. During this process, they sang the gravesongs that had been with Azulea's people since before they had come to the Shining City. The voices of the Great Archive rose over the desert, singing of their loss. They sang of sand and sky and how nothing persevered but Knowledge. They sang of generations to come and beseeched Amma to whisper her Knowledge onto them in their dreams. It was beautiful. Azulea hated every moment.

Azulea and Peny shuffled through the halls of the Archive. They were covered in dirt. Everyone moved as if in a daze. Azulea was glad that her cousin had cried herself out. Peny's arm clasped in her own, and only now did Azulea continue to hold the other girl's arm, more to give emotional support rather than receive guidance. She had no doubt Peny felt as she did, hollowed out. No feelings, not anger or sadness. Just empty.

"Azulea, can we talk?"

It was Garoq.

"Garoq, are you all right?" Peny asked, her words lilting up in surprise.

"He is hunched over and is terribly pale and has awful bags under his eyes," Peny said in an aside to Azulea. "All the feathers on his head are standing straight up."

"You do know I can hear you?"

"And he sounds irritable," Peny continued.

Azulea tried but failed to hide her smile. She pressed her lips tightly together. "I'm sorry. Is everything all right?" She could hear Garoq cracking his knuckles over and over, first the left hand, then the right, the feathers swishing in protest. No, this wasn't lighthearted Garoq who made alcohol in his classes.

Peny huffed. "That's what I asked."

"I need to talk to Azulea," Garoq said, curtly.

Peny didn't move.

"Alone."

Peny untwined her arm from Azulea's. "Fine. I've no need to stay where I'm not wanted."

"No, Peny," Azulea said, trying to interrupt her. It didn't work. Azulea and her mother used silence to manipulate conversations, while Peny used words. Lots and lots of words.

"Far be it from me to get in the way of romance."

Garoq and Azulea both groaned.

"...I'm just a lowly, lonely apprentice so buried in work that I am doomed to spend my life sad and alone."

"You've never slept alone in your life," Garoq snorted.

"Just let her go," Azulea said to Garoq. "If you interrupt too much, she'll just start her lament again from the beginning."

"I can hear you," Peny said, coming to the end of her monologue. "Now that I've made my point..." She kissed both Garoq and Azulea on each cheek. "I'm going to our study room. Training is supposed to start again tomorrow afternoon. I should get caught up on my reading."

"Thank you, Peny," Garoq added ungraciously.

Peny padded down the hall and was gone in seconds. There was a muttered comment from Garoq about feather-heads.

"She's not usually such a conscientious student," Azulea said. "We should consider ourselves lucky." She changed the subject, suspecting that Garoq had sought her out about the request she had made of him. Was that only last night?

"Azulea, at first, I didn't believe you, but now I don't know what to do."

His words lurched to a halt. Azulea could guess the expression on her face. No one had believed her. Wait, that wasn't true. Melehti had believed her. Without any evidence or proof, Melehti had taken Azulea's words as truth.

Garoq started again. "I'm sorry, but I didn't. It was so ludicrous. But I thought, why not? You're a friend. What could it hurt to run a few tests?"

He clasped Azulea's upper arms. He was so close she could smell the lemon and herb spices from his dinner and the slightly sour scent of an unwashed body. He must have been working nonstop.

"But the preliminary results do look like *Cinchona Aerium*." He spoke as if the weight of the world burdened him, and Azulea felt bad knowing that she had done this to him.

Garoq stumbled over the words. "I think, I think, if what you said was true, if this was on her clothing…then your grandmother, the matriarch, *was* murdered."

Azulea released a breath. She knew how he felt: as if saying the words made it real. She reached out to clasp his hands.

"Thank you." Azulea felt tears begin. "This is just what we need. Proof."

His hands tensed.

"Not yet." Garoq's voice was only a whisper of sound. "I need an actual sample to do a direct comparison. The Archive has none."

Azulea nodded, understanding. "I have some."

Garoq let go of her hands and took a step back.

"What is it?"

"Why would you have *Cinchona Aerium*? Why would you keep poison?"

Azulea tried not to let her voice betray her. "Because you keep notes and writings on what you learn. I am not so lucky. I, too, need to have things to help my memory."

Garoq's beak clacked once, and he drew in a breath as if to interrupt. Azulea held up a hand.

"Yes, like my grandmother, I can recall texts read decades ago, but it isn't perfect. I want to touch and smell and taste. I can remember everything, but my collection helps me recall faster and with more detail."

Garoq was unconvinced. "A poison?"

"You're an alchemist," Azulea said, trying to keep a grip on her patience. "Many things, including healing herbs, can become poisons when ingested in higher quantities. I'll get you your sample first thing tomorrow morning. You'll be in the laboratory?"

"Of course, but…"

"Tomorrow, then."

"We must do it tonight," Garoq insisted. "This is too important." His voice wavered.

Azulea took a step toward him and put a hand out. It landed on his shoulder where the bright green feathers faded to darker shades. He started as if nervous. She was not sure if he was afraid of her, of the killer, or of the very idea of what they were doing. She squeezed once. "It'll be all right."

"We must tell the Head Archivist, right away. She must know."

Azulea shook her head. "I told my mother my suspicions even before I brought the poison to you for testing." At her words, he relaxed a little. "We just need to complete the tests and get the evidence."

"Then we should get your sample immediately."

"When did you last sleep, Garoq?" Azulea asked.

He murmured something inaudible.

"What was that?" Azulea pressed.

"I haven't. Not since you gave me your robes."

Azulea let her hand drop to her side. "You need to get some rest, Garoq."

"But…"

He had started cracking his knuckles again. The sound made Azulea wince.

"You'd agree this is too important for any errors, right?"

He paused. "You're right."

She took his arm, he didn't start this time, and pushed him gently in the direction of his chambers. He lived on the far side of the Academy building. "Good. Go rest."

"And you'll get me the sample tomorrow? First thing in the morning?"

"Absolutely," Azulea said, her voice low and firm. "Then we will bring the resources and wrath of the entire Archive to find and punish this killer."

Azulea was awake the next morning well before the cock's crow. She didn't register much warmth from her window, and the sounds of the morning souq had yet to rise to the hubbub that signified the opening of stalls and raucous back-and-forth haggling that was the heart of any true market.

She dressed in record time and descended to the first floor. In the kitchens, she ate a bowl of fūl and a small loaf of bread sweetened with dates, honey, and figs. After she finished, Azulea pocketed a couple more of the small loaves. Friendly curses from Waud, the morning cook, followed her out of the kitchen, along with complaints that if other people wanted food they could damn well come down and get it themselves.

Azulea wove through the corridors. More and more people were arriving. The morning was beginning for the resident Archivists and their trader guests at the Archive. She, once again, avoided the Gallery Chamber where her grandmother had died and used a circuitous route to the study rooms.

There were many of these small rooms, little more than alcoves around the Archive and Academy. Individual Archivists kept personal copies of lectures, in-process manuscripts, inks and paints, and any other amount of paraphernalia critical to their work. Azulea shuddered to think of what Garoq kept in his. As neither of them was a full Archivist, Azulea and Peny shared one.

Unfortunately, Azulea added uncharitably, as she opened the door to the room and a rank musky odor wafted out, poorly hidden under what must have been a cloud of Peny's persimmon scent. Her nose wrinkled. It was terrible.

Azulea stumbled across the room. She cursed as she slipped on several rumpled blankets. She rubbed her shoulder for a second where she had jerked it as she tried to catch herself on the windowsill. The room was a mess.

"Come on, Peny! Were you *entertaining* in here?! In the study room?! You have a room of your own."

Disgusted, Azulea threw open the window and let the warm morning breeze waft through the room. She took a cautious sniff. At least it seemed to clear out most of the stink.

Azulea heard a giggle behind her. A musical voice murmured in response.

Azulea turned to face the doorway just as she heard them enter. She raised one of the blankets and shook it in the direction of the doorway. "Peny?"

The giggle stopped. "Oooh! Sorry, Azulea. I didn't know you'd be here this early."

"I assumed that."

There was an awkward silence followed by the shuffling of bodies as two people entered the small room.

"Who is your friend?" Azulea asked, slightly annoyed that Peny didn't identify who was with her.

"My apologies, gracious Azulea."

She frowned, trying to place the voice. "Davarr?"

"At your service," the Elishian said, his voice dropping in height in what Azulea assumed was a bow.

"Davarr has been helping me with my languages," Peny said, her voice breathless.

Azulea felt the blanket snatched from her fingers. Peny wandered over to the far side of the room. She picked up and moved several items. Tidying up.

Azulea winced, hearing a glass of liquid slosh. If the sound was any indication, Azulea had no doubt that in the near future, she would be finding sticky residue of whatever beverage Peny had been drinking.

Davarr took the large stuffed chair closest to the door. It was the one luxury in a room of hard wooden chairs, desks, cabinets, papers, and inks.

"This place is a terrible mess," Peny complained. "The pages I was copying of Hmuruni's Gate Protocols are scattered all over my desk."

Azulea didn't want to have this conversation in front of a stranger, especially not in front of a suspect in her grandmother's murder. She pasted a smile on her face. She hoped it didn't look as artificial as it felt. "I'll be out of here shortly. I just wanted to pick up something from my collection."

Peny answered in the affirmative. Davarr seemed content to sit quietly in the chair.

Peny was throwing papers and books across every desk

and surface on her side of the room. A litany of complaints came from her about the state of the room.

"It isn't like I made the mess," Azulea protested. While she wasn't particularly fond of Peny's alley cat ways, what she hated more was how often her cousin let their space fall into such disarray.

Azulea ran her fingers over a massive cabinet that covered an entire wall on her side of the room. It had dozens of small and large drawers. On each drawer was a label with tiny raised dots—her own writing system. Her grandmother had learned it from a trader who had been to the Parascotopetl world and then taught it to Azulea. Azulea found the drawer she was looking for, pulled it open, and reached in gingerly for the small vial inside.

"*Cinchona Aerium*. Are you planning a revelry?"

Azulea startled at Davarr's comment. She didn't realize anyone else other than she and her grandmother could read Parascotopetl.

As if understanding her surprise, the Elishian laughed, an odd watery sound. "Yes, I can read the language of the dark world."

"No. No revelry."

"Pity," Davarr continued. "I can see *Tabgh Leaf* labelled on the drawer by your right elbow. Together with *Cinchona*, I've heard it makes a wonderful smoke."

"Some other time," Azulea said, keeping her tone level. She was well aware of the mind-altering properties of that combination. She was still irked that Davarr had called her a cripple only two days earlier, and doubly annoyed that he and Peny were obviously using their shared study space for assignations. She was irritated with Peny, but that didn't mean she couldn't be irritated with Davarr too.

"Here. I brought breakfast," Azulea said curtly as she set the bread down, none too gently, on the open surface of her own desk. She felt a small satisfaction as she felt it squelch slightly under the force of her hand.

"I assume the room will be tidy by this evening," Azulea said over her shoulder as she exited. She heard a plaintive wail, "But I didn't do this…" as she descended the stairs that would take her to the main level and out to the central courtyard. "…at least, I don't think I did."

In her hand, Azulea held the vial of *Cinchona Aerium*. She hefted it thoughtfully, sifting through her memories for a comparison. Yes, it definitely felt lighter. She stopped dead. Could someone have used her own collection to poison her grandmother?

People passed Azulea on the path. She was crossing the large central courtyard between buildings. She was surrounded by family and friends, colleagues and classmates, and yet felt more alone than she had in a long time. Someone bumped her gently from behind.

"Well, look who I have the good fortune to run into. Literally."

Azulea pocketed the vial and turned to face the speaker. "Handsome Dan." She squinted. Handsome Dan was somewhat easier to identify as his pale skin made him stand out amongst the majority of the populace. In the bright morning sunlight, she could make out the outline of his body in what looked like a long, gold-colored jacket.

"And where are you going so early this morning?" Azulea kept her tone deliberately light. She started walking.

"No, I truly am not one for early mornings," he agreed, sidestepping her question. "But since I am up and my bed is too far away to sing to me, may I escort you to wherever you are headed?"

Azulea raised an eyebrow. "Such chivalry."

Handsome Dan made a rude noise. "Don't mock, dear. I am nothing if not gallant." He tucked her arm into his. "Now, where are we going?"

Azulea's fingers sank into the rich brocade. She couldn't help but let her fingers skim across the embossed cloth. It was studded with small, carefully shaped gemstones, medallions of enamel, as well as embroidery. Her brow furrowed as she tried to surreptitiously identify the pattern.

"It is a grove of blossoming peach trees," Handsome Dan said, answering her questing fingers.

Azulea slowed to let him match her pace. "Thank you. I'm going to the Academy to see Garoq. I have some questions for him." She paused for a heartbeat before continuing. "And a few questions for you, too."

She felt the muscles of his arm tighten under the heavy material. "So, you've decided to take me up on my offer?" His voice was hopeful.

Azulea shook her head. "I wanted to ask about the day before yesterday. You said you were in the Grand Parlor?"

"Hmm? Yes, brokering a deal with the Vlunder guilds." Azulea could hear the lie as it left his tongue.

She patted his arm in a friendly way. "I wish I had known you were there. It would've been so much easier with the quarrel. Why didn't you speak up?"

"I knew you had everything well in hand, Azulea. You know, I, like your grandmother, have always had faith in your abilities." His answer was quick. Too quick.

She shrugged. "I know the High Trade Pavilion was banned from the Archive. I can only hope the altercation has not caused them trouble."

"I doubt it. Very little troubles the Stone people. In fact, I find it hard to believe they would be involved in any kind of altercation." His steps slowed. "What are you really asking?"

"You weren't in the Grand Parlor." It wasn't a question.

There was a pause. "No. I wasn't."

"You were on the second floor by the stairs, not far from where Amma was murdered." Azulea fought to keep her voice level.

Handsome Dan was silent. No, he was more than that. He was utterly still. He walked beside her, but it was as if everything about him had turned inward. No sound of breath, no slight movements of body or muscle, even his tell-tale limp seemed to have disappeared. It was as if she walked next to a ghost, and his hand on her arm was the only tangible thing tethering him to this time and place.

There was an intake of breath as Dan seemed to come back to himself. He sucked on his teeth, the sound disturbing. "You are asking me if I killed your grandmother?"

"What were you doing there?" Azulea asked.

His grip tightened on her arm. Not quite painfully. Not yet. "None of your business. But if someone was willing to take another's life, to cut short their thread, and you thought that confronting that person all by yourself, with no support, was a good idea, then you are more reckless or more arrogant than I realized."

His fingers tightened even further, and he sped up his pace, dragging her down the path. Azulea recoiled as his long fingernails dug into her arm.

"I'll bet you haven't even told your suspicions to anyone."

Azulea's heart pounded in her chest. It was broad daylight, in an open courtyard. She could scream. She drew in a breath.

Dan shoved her none too gently against one of the Archive buildings. The cool indicated they were in shadow now. His voice was soft, casual. "Did you ever think about how easy it would be to dispose of *you*, Azulea?"

She felt a small sharp point against her side. A knife? All the color left her face.

"I see you understand."

Azulea felt him sheathe the knife that she never even heard him draw. One second it was there, and then it was gone.

"Besides," he brought his lips to where she could feel them brush her ear, his words only the barest whisper of sound, "you'd have to prove it."

He straightened and let go of her arm. It was such a shock that it took Azulea a moment to catch her balance. In a voice, much more jovial and significantly louder, he spoke. "I believe this is where you were headed. The door is to your right," he added. "I'll bid you good day, Azulea. Think about what I said. And be careful."

Then, he was gone.

She tried not to pant. Sweat clung to her, sticky and cool. Azulea leaned against the wide doorway, trying to regain her equilibrium. Students and scholars flowed past her in and out of the building, laughing, chatting, or silent, their minds perhaps on studies or research. She stood there, an island of muddy emotion. She could smell her own fear. What had she been thinking?

Azulea mentally shook herself and forced her hands to stop trembling. *It is over. And Handsome Dan didn't kill you.* She didn't know what it meant, but she'd save his words, and warning, to process later. She patted her pocket to assure herself that the vial was still safe, and gripping her cane more firmly, strode down the hall to Garoq's lab.

This time, Azulea didn't bother to knock at the door to the lab. She let herself in. She closed the door carefully behind her. There was a scent in the air—alcohol, and something else, a faint musky scent. *If Garoq has been imbibing already this morning...* Azulea didn't finish the angry thought as she maneuvered through the lab, her hands brushing tables as she passed. Ahead she could hear gasping and muttering. There was a stumble and then a crash. She heard glass break.

"Garoq?" Azulea called out. "Garoq, if you are drunk, I swe..."

Her words were cut off as she heard scrabbling and scratching and papers crinkling. Then a body slammed against something heavy and thudded to the floor.

"Garoq?" Azulea sped up, and under her sandals, she felt the flooring change from smooth wood to grit and liquid. She stepped carefully, wary of slipping.

"Garoq, are you all right?" She could feel shards of ceramic under her sandals and papers rustle as she slid her feet forward, one step at a time. As she drew closer to the far end of the lab, where they had spoken, there was more and more disarray. Her hands brushed tables that were overturned and whatever experiments had been in process, smashed and strewn widely. She wiped her fingers on her robe. Liquid sucked at Azulea's sandals, and the overwhelming scent of singed feathers and cooked meat assaulted her.

"Get away!" The words were thin and strained, like a lute strung too taut, as if the notes would break. It was followed by a series of gasps and wheezes.

Azulea turned toward the voice. "Garoq? Answer me! Let me help." She slowed her pace even more, liquid spattered her feet, but she continued her forward movement. "Who did this?"

Her only answer was a series of barking coughs.

Garoq was on the floor, his limbs flailing in spastic motions, his beak digging into the wooden floorboards. The stench of burning was overwhelming. Under it, mixed with the smell of chemicals and alcohol, Azulea smelled blood and excrement. This wasn't an accident.

She tensed at the thought, her heart picking up speed. The killer must have attacked Garoq. What did they do to him? Azulea knelt and put a hand cautiously on Garoq's back. It was hot. Not just warm or fevered but burning hot.

"No!" The words were strangled.

Garoq threw her hand off of him with such ferocity, Azulea fell backward. She hissed as her left hand came down in broken glass.

He was scrambling, trying to get to his webbed feet. Azulea could feel his movements. It was like standing in front of one of the clay ovens in the kitchen. He radiated heat like a fire.

Azulea stood. Careful of her hand, she reached out and caught a handful of Garoq's robe. With her good right hand, she hauled him to his feet. He stumbled against her. Automatically, Azulea's hands wrapped around to steady him. They both screamed at her touch.

Garoq was literally burning, and when Azulea had grasped him, pieces of his flesh and feathers came off. Charred and peeling, it stuck to her skin.

"Oh gods of hearth and…fuck!" They broke apart.

A leather notebook with papers sticking out around the edges was thrust into her hands. The corners already curling from the heat. Azulea screamed in pain as it came in contact with her hands.

All around there was the crackle and pop of flames. Smoke was filling the room as materials ignited. Azulea coughed and clutched the documents to her chest. "Garoq?" It was getting hard to breathe, but she couldn't leave Garoq like this.

"The well." She put a hand out but didn't touch him. As

soon as the words were out of her mouth, Azulea knew it wouldn't work. The well was on the far side of the building, and the combustion was too fast. He was burning alive right in front of her.

"Too late." The words were almost unrecognizable. "Driiiink."

A gust of heat hit her. Azulea put an arm up to shield her face and took an involuntary step back. She smelled her own hair burning.

Garoq made a thin, high-pitched keen that shot right through her. The accompanying blast of heat as more of his body ignited forced her farther and farther back. Her good friend was dying horribly, and there was nothing Azulea could do.

She couldn't bring herself to leave Garoq, not until his screaming finally stopped. She ran. The heat behind her was increasing, and she remembered, too late, about Garoq's alembic with his ersatz Thujone liquor... She didn't even finish the thought before an explosion ripped the air around her and she was thrown forward, through the door and into the hallway.

She crumpled, half conscious. The journal was still wrapped in her burned and bleeding hands. She heard shouts of "Fire!" and a call for buckets. Archivists and academicians, students and traders rushed past as Azulea stumbled to her feet. Anonymous hands helped her up and out of the building where she sputtered and coughed and gasped in the morning air.

"Kesa mak?"

Azulea blinked repeatedly and kept trying to clear her throat. Her eyes ran. Her nose ran. She struggled to place the voice. Scaled fingers pressed a wet cloth into her hands. It was Mosa, the Lacerti. Their scaled bodies made them highly immune to fire.

She nodded gratefully in his direction. Yes, she was fine, but she didn't attempt to speak. The Lacerti language would be too much right now. The lizard-man left, promising to find her medical attention.

Azulea rubbed the soot on her face. The fine powder was caught in the creases of her skin. Tears tracked down her cheeks, and she couldn't catch her breath. Her skin was warm and tight, as if sunburnt, and her arms tingled where she had come in contact with Garoq. She imagined that she looked a fright with the burns. But it was nothing compared to what had happened to him.

Garoq was dead. He had been murdered horrifically because she had asked him for help. Azulea choked as a sob escaped her dry throat. She shunted away her emotions before they overwhelmed her. She couldn't do this. Not here, not now. She shoved the scorched journal into her robe and got to her feet.

A bucket line had already begun, people side by side, voices shouting to each other as they passed buckets of water from one hand to the next to put out the blaze. Fire. Her heart dropped. There was nothing so devastating to any repository of knowledge as fire. Azulea stepped into the line, joining in the effort. She tried not to think about Garoq, about what happened to him. It was too awful. Afterward, she would talk to her mother. This time, there would be no doubt as to the malicious activity taking place in the walls of the Archive.

Azulea's arms ached. Her back ached. Her face itched, and she had blisters on her hands. Not only from the fire, but also from passing heavy buckets back and forth for hours. The conflagration had risen fast in the dry summer air, and a light wind had swept it through the classroom buildings as swiftly as wildfire. After the first hour, they had given up on the Academy and instead began using the water to soak down the Residence and the flanking Archive Repositories.

"Hold still, Azulea," Otha snapped, as she dabbed at Azulea's face with a heavy cream. The greasy substance was cooling and soothed the tight warmth on her cheeks. Her arms and right hand were already covered with it. The cuts from the glass on her left hand had thankfully been shallow, and she wriggled her fingers in the light bandage. "Stop that," Otha said, not even pausing as she continued to apply the cream. "You are very lucky it isn't more serious."

Other than Garoq, no one had been killed. Around her, in the infirmary, several other people were receiving care for minor burns and abrasions, plus one sprained ankle from a student who had tripped in her rush to evacuate the Academy building.

"I don't know about lucky," Azulea said, feeling the weight of the book in her robes. The cracked leather cover bristled against her skin, the pebbled texture a constant reminder of what the information within had cost. She struggled to maintain her composure.

As if sensing the younger woman's frame of mind, Otha stopped and gingerly wrapped her arms around Azulea, mindful of the burns and blisters. "It is a terrible thing, what has happened, but I am grateful to have you safe."

Azulea nodded. "I know." She paused. "You know it was not an accident, right?" Her voice broke on the words.

Otha's own voice was unsteady as she picked anxiously at Azulea's robes. "Water wasn't effective. Not on the Academy building. The flames took far too long to be extinguished. The fire fought back, like a living thing. Too many people have remarked on that."

Azulea choked up. Her throat was too tight to describe what she had been privy to.

Otha continued, sounding lost. "I don't know how this happened or the details or what it means, but everyone knows the fire was intentional. Even while we were still dousing the buildings and trying to contain the blaze, Hypatia shut down all the gates to the Labyrinth. She placed guards on the buildings, and no one is permitted to leave."

"I need to talk to my mother."

"Right now might not be the best…"

"I know who started the fire."

Otha rocked back. There was a suppressed sound of horror from the other woman.

"Well, maybe not who, but I know why. They killed Garoq." Azulea had had a lot of time to think while passing buckets back and forth. No matter how hard she tried she could not escape the vision of Garoq's death or his last words. He had mentioned "drink." It was important. If she were dying, what would she say? If she had just one word? She would give some indication as to her killer or how she was killed. *Drink.* Azulea scanned her mind, trying to recall if there was anything she could remember, any drink that could cause a body to spontaneously combust.

There was something, teasing at the edges of her mind. Her grandmother had talked about something similar: *exothermic internal chemical reactions.* Amma had been Head Archivist at the time. But she hadn't been talking to Azulea. Azulea was three-years-old and sitting on her grandmother's lap playing with her necklace.

Azulea couldn't help but smile at the memory. She remembered how smooth the pearls felt as she ran them between her fingers, noting the slight imperfections in shape and size.

Azulea rubbed the bandaged palm of her left hand to her

eye. It was so frustrating. She winced as she ground the grit and dirt into her tender eyelids. It was so very long ago. She remembered the grave notes and angry undercurrent in her grandmother's usually calm voice. Even as a child, she had noticed the tension.

Azulea sounded out the words in her head as she tried to put an adult understanding to the childhood memory. *Thermal runaway. Four grades of aldehyde.* It wasn't a drink that Garoq had been referring to but something someone had put in his drink.

She struggled to recall the name, words dancing through her mind like butterflies as she struggled to capture the right one. Conflagration. Jewel. Sulphur. Acetone. Explosion. Fire. Stone. Fire Stone. Fire Opal. *Opalis Incendium*. That was it! The gemstone was fragile and explosive, and crumbled up in a powder, could be hidden anywhere. What made it particularly distasteful was that it didn't activate until it came in contact with the enzymes in a living body. After that, there was nothing anyone could do. A chain reaction was set in motion. The compound had turned Garoq's entire body into a fiery candle, burning the very fat from his flesh and keeping him alive long enough to do it.

Azulea shuddered. She came back to herself and realized that Otha had asked her a question. Twice.

"Why, Azulea?"

Azulea tried to shrug back into her robes, but the cream and bandages made it awkward. "It's my fault."

"I don't believe that." Otha slapped away Azulea's hands and pulled the clothing back up on the younger woman's shoulders, tucking the singed ends in.

Azulea stiffened.

"No, you couldn't do it yourself," Otha said, as if hearing Azulea's thoughts. "The cream."

Azulea ignored her aunt's words. She slid off the cot. "I

must speak to my mother, right away. Garoq had proof that Grandmother was murdered."

"No."

Azulea didn't have the time or mental energy to explain herself again. "It's true," she said flatly. "I have to go."

Azulea's cane had been lost, but she didn't need it indoors. Placing her tender hand hesitantly on the wall, Azulea hurried out of the Infirmary. She ignored Otha's calls behind her.

As she passed through the buildings, Azulea noted the subdued air. People walked swiftly, alone or in small groups, saying little. Even inside, the smell of smoke was everywhere. Or was that just her own clothing and hair? As she continued, fewer and fewer people were evident—not traders, not archivists, not academicians or students. She made her way up the ramp into the main building where her mother's office was and blundered into a man. He had been standing motionless. Silent. Tall, well-muscled and practically vibrating with tension. Azulea pushed away, embarrassed. She hadn't expected to find a guard. Nor the large spear he held. After a plethora of apologies, she continued. Now she moved even slower, trying to sense if there were others stationed around the building. If her mother had not believed in danger to the Archive before, then she definitely believed in it now. From the entrance of the building to the hallway leading to the Head Archivist's office, Azulea counted at least four guards. She had no doubt there were others she hadn't noticed.

But where the rest of the Archive's campus was quiet, the Residency area was loud. Angry merchants and traders filled the hallway leading to her mother's office. It was easy to understand their frustration.

"I was supposed to leave yesterday with the tide winds. The Archivist does us pain."

Azulea recognized the harsh Lacerti language. It was Mosa, and he was angry. He was stringing together words almost faster than even she could understand.

"Yesterday, I wait, to honor your Book-Goddess. Today, I help with dangerous fire, and now you refuse my journey. Our goods rot in the warehouse!"

His complaints were not very different from the dozen or so other trade representatives.

Azulea pushed her way past Mosa who barked at her, demanding she, "Tell them. Tell them right, or Mosa leave." She plastered a supportive yet noncommittal look on her face and kept moving. She bumped into two other merchants and a third who was shouting as he was escorted back to his room by a pair of guards. The atmosphere in the hallway was turning into something ugly.

Up ahead, Viera was placating the emissary from the Andive merchants of Kyrea, and assuaging the fears of a group of field scholars who had been visiting from the House of Wisdom.

Azulea did her best to ignore all of this as she came abreast of the door to the Head Archivist's office.

A throat cleared. "Uh, Archivist? You may not pass any farther."

Another guard. He sounded young. Azulea strode right past him.

He hurried to catch up with her and then scrambled to put himself between Azulea and the door to the Head Archivist's office. She stopped and lifted her face up to his. She heard the uncomfortable intake of breath.

"I'm here on an urgent matter for the Head Archivist," Azulea said, each word dropping like a stone. She didn't recognize the young man's voice. The Archive with all its parts—the Residence, the Academy, and the Archive's Repository where the actually documents were stored—was huge, with hundreds of people working, teaching, and living on the grounds. But she did recognize his discomfort with stopping her.

Drawing her confidence around her like a robe, Azulea kept her tone cool, as if explaining herself to him was one more annoyance than she could bear. "My mother will be expecting me."

"Oh? Oh!"

Azulea didn't respond. She kept her expression neutral and didn't let her gaze stray from where she assumed his face was.

"Uh, I guess that's all right, then."

Azulea nodded firmly. "Thank you…?" She let her words trail off.

"Mikkal. It's Mikkal. I started working for the Superintendent a month ago," he said, his words filling the silence Azulea had left.

Azulea hid her surprise. Charemon had hired guards a month ago? She nodded again and made a noncommittal noise. With that she turned toward the door, dismissing the guard. "Thank you, Mikkal."

"Uh, I'm going to go back to my post now," he stuttered. Azulea could hear his sandals as he slapped back toward the entrance to the hallway.

Azulea put her hand to her mother's office door but stopped at hearing raised voices inside. It was Charemon and her mother. Azulea frowned. Her mother never raised her voice, and Charemon was always unfailingly polite and deferential. She leaned closer to listen.

"I tell you, no! We cannot let this continue. The Residence is full of angry traders. They are furious that we have shut down the gates, offended that we have set guards to watch them, and worst, that you are costing them money."

"Charemon, stop! I know this."

Azulea could picture her mother, fingers pinching the bridge of her nose as she tried to come up with the answer to some difficult question.

"Hypatia, you must listen to me. The Lacerti are dangerous. Your mother banned Mosa and his people more than fifty years ago when they destroyed several Archive buildings the first time. Now they've done it again."

"But we don't know that the Lacerti caused this fire."

Charemon's exclamation was filled with incredulity. "Are you as blind and daft as Azulea? He was there! In the Academy!"

"I'll thank you to not speak so of my daughter, Charemon. You are a dear friend, and I value your counsel, but that is not a line to cross."

There was an exhalation of breath and the sound of heavy footfalls. "Forgive me, Hypatia. But you allowed Amma to coddle her. Azulea has fanciful ideas in her head."

Azulea bristled.

"And what if she's right?"

Was that her mother? Standing up for her? The woman who demanded perfection? Azulea's heart rose.

"That someone murdered Amma?" There was a sound of derision. "Mark my words, this won't end well."

"Your objections have been noted." The chill in her mother's voice came through the wood. "You think I don't have my own doubts. Every report you have given me about Azulea's progress as a student of the Archive…but, I promised my mother that I would give her the chance…"

"To what? Fail? Oh Hypatia, it is cruel." The words dripped with a sincerity that made Azulea itch.

"You know, little girls who listen at doors never hear well of themselves." The voice came from behind her.

Azulea straightened with a start. Her first response, to deny that was what she was doing, was foolish. However, eavesdropping was exactly what she had been doing. She scowled and opted for the simplest choice. "Good afternoon, Melehti. Why are you here?"

"To the point as always," Melehti said, sarcasm coloring her voice. There was a pause. "What happened to you?"

Azulea felt Melehti take her hand and turn it over, gently running her fingers over the burned skin, careful of the poultice.

"I'm fine."

"I heard about the fire."

"Is that why you're here?" Azulea asked. Melehti's fingers felt good as they traced over her bandaged palms, and then paused at her wrist as if feeling for her pulse before moving back down to her fingers.

"No."

The muscular hands let go, and Azulea curled her fingers into her robe, ignoring the smears of poultice she was leaving on the clothing.

"You're here about the murder! You said you would give me time." Azulea hated the whine in her voice.

Melehti rapped sharply on the door. "Is that how little you think of me, Azulea? Truly?"

Azulea suppressed her first sarcastic reply. She turned her face away. "I'm sorr…"

"No, you're not." Melehti knocked again. Harder, her anger expressing itself in violent booming blows that vibrated down the corridor. "You're willing to trust Peny, but not me. You'll work with her, but not me. Do you know why?"

Azulea didn't offer a rejoinder. She shook her head and

wrapped her arms around herself. Why was she afraid to hear Melehti's answer to the question?

"Because you can control her."

"That's not true!"

The whispered exclamation was lost as the door was yanked open.

"What?!" Charemon was breathing heavily.

Azulea heard the click in the back of Melehti's throat that signaled her irritation.

"I'm here to see the Head Archivist."

"She's otherwise occupied. If you had not heard, there has been a fire." Azulea could feel Charemon's gaze rove over both of them. "There was a guard."

Azulea raised an eyebrow. "You mean Mikkal?" She was certainly unimpressed with Charemon's choice of security personnel.

Melehti snorted, much less diplomatic by nature. "I pulled my knife, and he almost wet himself."

She stepped forward, chest to chest with Charemon. "I'm here from the Governor. I am tired of waiting. Announce us."

Charemon *hmm'd*.

Azulea could tell he had not liked being ordered to do Melehti's bidding. She doubted there were many who told him what to do.

"As Superintendent, perhaps I can…"

Melehti swept her arm in a cutting gesture. "No. The Head Archivist."

Charemon *hmm'd* again.

"It's all right, Charemon," came a voice from behind him. "I'm not some wilting flower to be protected, and I'm sure there is much to discuss."

The older man stepped to the side, but not fully ceding the doorway. Melehti stalked past him, the onyx horns on her head faintly scraping the top of the doorframe. She didn't pause or apologize.

Azulea moved to follow. She heard the door begin to close. She was going to be left to wait in the hall. She glowered.

"Thank you, Charemon." She brought her hand up to catch the door before it closed completely. "I appreciate the opportunity to speak with my mother." She shouldered through the narrowing gap, ignoring the pain in her hand and shoulder.

Charemon *hmm'd*. Azulea ignored him.

Hypatia was behind her desk. She stood abruptly, the heavy wooden chair scraping backward over the stone floor with an audible shriek.

Azulea came abreast of Melehti. "You didn't wait." The statement wasn't an accusation so much as a compliment.

Melehti didn't glance at her. "You didn't need me to."

Azulea swallowed, feeling stupid. "Thank you." The words were small, timid things.

"For what?" Melehti sounded surprised.

Their conversation was interrupted by Azulea's mother who had come around the desk to pull her daughter up and envelop her in a tight embrace.

Azulea hugged her back. The Head Archivist reeked of sweat and smoke. Her robes were still damp from the bucket lines. Azulea had no doubt that she smelled no better, with many of the same aromas. She couldn't get the smell of burnt flesh and singed hair out of her nostrils.

"I am so glad you are safe," her mother murmured into Azulea's hair. "Your hands…"

"Will heal," Azulea said.

Charemon stepped into the office. His body was a palpable presence behind them. He *hmm'd*. Melehti stiffened.

Azulea sensed rather than heard the faint rustle of Melehti's hand going to the knife at her waist.

There was a pained sigh from Hypatia as she released Azulea and stepped back. "Charemon, would you get us some kahwa?"

Her mother sounded defeated.

Azulea wondered if she imagined the faintest hesitation in the older man before he bowed and exited the room with a polite, "Of course, Head Archivist."

"That won't be necessary," Melehti interrupted, drawing a surprised look from both Charemon and the Head Archivist.

"Then Charemon, why don't you take a seat? I believe you're making our military-minded guest nervous," Hypatia said pointedly.

"I'm not going to stab you in the back, girl," Charemon said with an indignant huff. He dropped heavily into the seat opposite the door.

"Now," Hypatia said, circling the desk and settling back into her chair, all softness gone. "To what do I owe the honor of your presence, Arbiter?"

Melehti leaned forward, matching Hypatia's tone. "I come with condolences and an offer of assistance from the Governor during these trying times."

Hypatia didn't say anything.

Azulea knew what her mother was doing. Only a few days ago she had witnessed her mother use charm to manage the emotions and actions of Melehti and Davarr. Today, she had chosen a different dynamic; this one was of reserved, unimpeachable authority.

Melehti drummed fingers on the hilt of her knife. "He offers his prayers to those injured." Melehti swallowed. She was definitely not comfortable in this diplomatic role. "He also offers his Arbiter and twenty of his best men and women to supplement your own security."

"That is very generous of him," Hypatia said slowly. "But I believe we have matters well in hand."

Azulea could not detect even a hint of irony. For as long as she could remember, there had been a power struggle between the Governors of the Shining City and the Archive regarding the latter's complete independence from City administration and oversight.

Melehti snorted scornfully. "There were rumors of Lacerti…" Melehti let the words trail off, clearly baiting the Head Archivist.

"We will investigate, and when we discover the arsonist, we will see to his punishment." The words were impassive, but Azulea thought she heard some underlying emotion. She just could not discern what. "We do not jump to conclusions based on a trader's race."

"Of course," Melehti said quickly. "The Governor only asks to be kept informed."

"I understand."

Melehti hesitated, recognizing that perhaps the response didn't really promise the desired action. She shrugged. "I do have one other matter."

"Oh?"

Azulea held her breath.

There was a crackle of sound as Melehti set a sheaf of papers on the desk. The aged yellow sheets were a stark contrast to the dark desk surface. The Head Archivist leaned forward as the Arbiter smoothed out the crumpled sheets.

"This may be related. We recovered these pages from a raid on a Dark Hand smuggler. We believe they are from one of your books."

Azulea gasped and felt Melehti rigid next to her.

"I know this one. It has one of Viera's illuminations painted on the border," Hypatia said. "Her work is unmistakable."

"We have a thief in the Archive?" Azulea said, stunned at the revelation.

Melehti continued. "And not a very clever one considering they are selling it in the souq. It would only be a matter of time before someone notified you."

Charemon stood, startling everyone. "I would see to this at once, Head Archivist."

"Thank you, Charemon," Azulea's mother said. "If that is all, Arbiter, we will send word…"

"Actually," Azulea felt three pairs of eyes turn to her, "I have something to say. And I think all three of you need to hear it. Sit down. Please," she added after a second.

Azulea pulled the scorched leather book from inside her robe. "This came from Garoq, and it is proof of Amma's murder."

"No."

"Not in front of an outsider!"

Her mother and Charemon's objections came simultaneously.

"The Arbiter should know this."

"The Arbiter, or the lover?" Charemon's attack was unflinching.

Azulea's fingers tightened on the book. She gritted her teeth. She had spent so many years working and studying within the hierarchy of the Archive. Other than her demand to be an Archivist, she had never once questioned the system.

"This isn't her place, Azulea," her mother said, softly.

"This is exactly her place. Two people have died. They were killed, their lives taken from them." Azulea turned toward Charemon, earnest. "I know that you believe that Archive matters should remain within the Archive, but," Azulea took a deep breath, "but Melehti and her guards have experience."

Her mother and Charemon both started to form words. Azulea cut them off.

"No." Azulea's voice was still harsh with smoke. She coughed and cleared her throat. "When was the last time anyone in the Archive actually investigated a murder? Ever?"

The emotional currents in the room swirled around her so violently she could feel them as clearly as she could feel the misting air on an afternoon in the rainy season.

Azulea paused to make sure she had everyone's attention and then drove her point home. "Melehti and her soldiers have done this before, and if we want to actually catch this killer, we cannot stand on our pride."

It was the hardest thing Azulea had ever done in her life, to sit and remain silent and calm after that speech. Seconds passed. She couldn't even hear people breathing.

Finally, Charemon made a disgusted sound. He tossed his bulk back further into the chair and uttered a disgruntled agreement. It was a better acknowledgement than she had expected from the old man.

She waited for her mother to answer. A second ticked by. Then another. Her mother's voice was firm when she finally spoke. "Show us what you found."

Azulea stood and stretched, her back cracking alarmingly. They were all seated around a low table in her mother's office.

"I don't even know that word," Melehti said. She made a face. She had struggled to keep up with Hypatia, Charemon, and even Azulea as they perused Garoq's notes.

The book lay open in front of them. It stank of smoke, burned flesh, and charred leather. The pages were brittle and tended to crumble, even when handled carefully.

They had quickly found his notes stuffed inside, confirming Azulea's suspicion that the previous Head Archivist, her grandmother, had definitely been poisoned with *Cinchona Aerium*. Azulea couldn't help but tear up at the thought. Her eyes were irritated, and the tears soothed the ache, though it did little for the one in her heart.

Garoq had discovered a second chemical compound in the powder. He had been able to write down its various reactions with other biologicals but had not yet written down its name.

Hypatia, revered for her ability to be implacable, expressed frustration in the tiny, jerky movements of her body.

"Euderus," she said, sounding out the name. "It is a world. I don't think the direct gate to it has been opened in decades."

Charemon *hmm'd* in assent. "It is a wild world of high magic, significant danger, and little to encourage an active trade route."

"Look, here under this scorch mark. Something is underlined." Melehti was seated next to Azulea.

The table was small, and Azulea felt the other woman's thigh against her own. Melehti struggled to read the word. "Or...no, opt...no, Ophi...Ophiocor—"

"Cordyceps?" Azulea completed. She sat bolt upright/ "Ophiocordyceps?!"

"Yes. I think that may be what it says."

Azulea put a horrified hand to her throat. "The Corpse Plague."

"That can't be right," Hypatia said. Her voice thin and high. "It hasn't been seen in years."

Sensing something amiss, Melehti's follow-up was swift. "What's wrong?"

"Read me Garoq's test results again," Azulea demanded, formulas turning over in her mind.

Charemon leaned against the table, bending low over it. He repeated the results, reading each number slowly and clearly.

At the end, Azulea nodded. "Trust me, it matches. You know I don't forget anything. It is Ophiocordyceps, the Corpse Bloom."

Charemon cursed and quickly headed to the door, shouting for guards and Archivists.

"They infected Amma with spores from the Corpse Bloom," Azulea repeated, stunned.

"We have to get to the grave and hope it's not too late." Hypatia rose from the table. "Charemon, tell them to bring torches and tar."

Melehti gripped Azulea's hand so tightly the burns all but sparked over her skin. "I need someone to explain this to me. Now."

Azulea gasped out, "It's a parasitic spore. Tiny. It was in the powder that was put on my grandmother."

"I can understand that much," Melehti said thickly. "What I don't know is what it does."

"It makes you sick. Most people recover from it, but if you die, it takes over the body in a terrible way. It moves the corpse like a living puppet, and inside it is reproducing, like a virus, turning the dead into a bulbous capsule full of spores. It forces the body to go to the largest nearby heat source, sometimes a home or a shop. There, the spores explode from the body and infect even more people. Corpse Bloom Plague."

Hypatia and Charemon had bolted from the office.

Melehti's focus was intense. "How do I kill it?"

"Burn the body. Heat kills the spores."

Melehti stood. "I must go. More than just the Archive is in danger."

Azulea nodded. "It takes about two days for the parasite

to completely take over, and it can only manipulate the tissues for a few hours after that before it bursts. Never more than a day."

She tried to keep her explanation cool and logical to avoid the emotional upwelling. The murderer had not only killed her grandmother but had defiled her body in the most egregious way.

Azulea bowed her head as grief rode over her like a wave. It was crushing and suffocating. "Amma will have crawled out of her grave today." She clasped her hands on the table, the pain from her burns bringing her back.

Melehti knelt by Azulea and put a hand on her thigh. It was cool against Azulea's still overwarm skin. "I'll find her. I promise. I'll return her to rest. Don't cry, Azulea. I don't know what to do when you cry."

Azulea wiped away the tears that had gathered. "I'm fine. Find her. And after this, promise me we will find the wretched individual who did this to her."

"I promise."

She heard Melehti rush out the door, calling for her guards. Azulea listened to the sound of the Archive being roused. It wasn't a full alarm, but there was no mistaking the urgency of the summons.

She leaned back in the chair and closed her eyes. She felt deflated. Here she was, like so many times before, left behind again. As a blind woman, she couldn't hunt down a Corpse Bloom carrier. There was nothing more she could do. She put her head in her hands and let the despair rise.

※

Even though it felt like hours had passed, only a few minutes later, Azulea heard heavy steps coming down the hall. They turned into the office.

"Azulea?" It was Charemon. "What are you still doing here?"

She quickly wiped her face on her sleeve and grimaced, remembering too late the ash and smoke. No doubt she had smeared detritus all over her face. "Nothing," she said, embarrassed by the faint tremor in her voice.

Charemon approached. "The Head Archivist and the Arbiter with her soldiers have gone."

"I know. I just wish there was something I could do."

She heard the old man *hmm* in his peculiar way. "The Archive's greatest power is its people. Each is a single unit of independent strength and wisdom."

Azulea flinched. She never worked alone. She always had to rely on others.

Charemon didn't pause. She could feel him towering over her. Even in his seventh decade, the Superintendent was still an intimidating figure. "We will find your Amma, and we will capture this murderer."

Azulea felt terrible. How could she be so selfish? She was thinking about her own feelings of being left out. Had she forgotten that this was about her grandmother and Garoq?

"You're right, Charemon. Thank you."

Azulea levered herself to her feet. She trudged past him. "Anything that needs to be done, I can accomplish on my own."

Tucked into her robes were the illuminated pages that Melehti had left on the Head Archivist's desk.

"Azulea?" Charemon said placidly to her as she reached the door. "Don't lose those."

Azulea balled her fists and nodded. "I won't let you down." She couldn't hunt down a body, but perhaps she could discover something from the stolen manuscript pages.

Once in her room, Azulea dropped the pages on her small desk. She had intended to start immediately, but feeling exhausted and filthy and emotionally wrung out, she let her clothes fall where they might and disappeared into the adjoining baths. Just a quick bath. Once refreshed, she could try and find a solution.

Most rooms shared common baths. Azulea breathed a sigh of relief that no one else was in the room. She slid into the cool water. It immediately eased the burns on her skin, and her muscles loosened in the gentle whirlpools.

She had not intended to doze off, but the next thing Azulea heard was Peny. "Azulea? Are you in here?"

She roused herself, groggy and unsure how much time had passed. She got up from the bath and wrapped a towel around herself. "I'm here. What is it? Have they found Amma's body?" She hurried out of the water, slipping on the wet tile in her urgency.

"Not yet. They only left a little while ago."

Slowing to a safer speed, Azulea walked back toward her room. Peny followed, a shadow in her wake. Azulea could smell the persimmon.

"I wanted to know that you were okay. You know, after the fire?"

"I'm fine," Azulea said, scrubbing at her hair. She tended to avoid getting the tight curls wet more than once a week.

"No, you're not. You're angry. And I can see the blisters on your arms." Peny took Azulea's left hand and turned it over, looking at the cuts. "Let me help you bandage it."

Azulea yanked her hand back. "I can take care of it myself," she said stiffly. "Why does everyone feel like they have to grab me? I am perfectly capable."

"I didn't mean anything," Peny said in hurt and confusion.

Azulea pinched the bridge of her nose between her

fingers. Remembering it was her mother's trademark gesture, she dropped her hand. "I meant…thank you, Peny."

"What's wrong? I'm not a feather-head. You can tell me."

"Nothing's wrong," Azulea said, pulling out a fresh cloth to wrap her left hand. "I was just reminded that I rely on you."

"Well, of course!" Peny broke in. "Don't be ridiculous. We're family."

"Too much."

"Oh."

Azulea clumsily wrapped her cut hand and, going to her wardrobe, pulled out a summer robe. The idea of longer sleeves on her burned arms made her shudder.

She half turned. "That's all you have to say?"

"It was your mother, right?" Peny's words were flat and emotionless. "Or Charemon or some other stuck-in-the-old-ways Archivist going on and on about the vaunted craft of the Archivists? About how we are the sole bearers of culture and wisdom?"

Azulea's own mind repeated what she and Peny and all the other trainees had been taught. *Each Archivist carries the mission of the Archive and with their skills can capture the true knowledge of the Labyrinth, the worlds, the histories, and the people.*

"The Storytellers of worlds," Azulea murmured.

"They finally made you quit."

Azulea shook her head. "No."

"Then you're quitting on me." Peny was crying now. "We've worked together for three years. You are the one who wanted so badly to be an Archivist. Now I do, too. This is our dream!"

"I'm sorry," Azulea said. She found she'd been saying that a lot lately. "What we're doing, teaming up to do the work, making up for each other, it-it-it isn't right."

She walked to the door to her room and opened it. "If we want to succeed, we have to be able to stand alone."

"For someone so smart, you really are stupid," Peny bawled as she ran from the room.

≈

"Where's your cousin?"

Handsome Dan came up beside Azulea and bumped her gently. There was no way for Azulea to have sensed his approach in the souq. The noise of merchants and traders closing up their shops for the evening filled her ears. Then again, she never sensed his approach. The bright gold of his brocade jacket identified him, even in the waning light.

"At the Archive. Are you here to threaten me again?" Azulea said archly.

"Ah, Zuzu, I never threaten," he said lightly as he fell into step beside her. "I was merely warning you about the dangerous path you were on."

"This is the third time you have 'accidentally' bumped into me," she accused.

"How many times would be enough for you to consider it might not be by mere chance?" he answered cheerfully.

"You're following me? Why?" Azulea asked bluntly.

Handsome Dan shrugged. "A foolish promise I made too many years ago." He deftly helped himself to a piece of fruit from a stall as they walked by. His movements were swift but not so subtle that Azulea, so close to him, didn't notice.

"You should pay for that," Azulea said offhandedly.

He took a bite, crunching loudly with satisfaction. "Why? No one saw me do it. Not even you. So it never happened. But tell me, why are you here? The Archive has closed all the gates to the Labyrinth, the Head Archivist and the Arbiter have run off on some urgent quest. I would think you would be more..."

"Involved?" Azulea said bitterly.

"I was going to say 'angry,' but I guess that'll do. I know, whatever it is, it is about your grandmother. What is going on?"

Azulea stopped, considering.

"I would not recommend accusing me of her death again," Dan said quietly. What was that? Azulea would have sworn that nothing could shake the caravan captain, but the sorrow that wove between his words was a palpable thing, raw and feral.

"You didn't kill her," Azulea breathed.

"I knew her since she was a little girl." There was a smile in his words. "My people are much longer lived than yours. I had hoped she would journey the Labyrinth with me, but it wasn't to be."

He sighed. It was half heartfelt and half overly dramatic. An impressive feat.

"And now?"

"And now, I will find out who murdered her and ensure their death is painful and slow."

Azulea shuddered. This Dan was not the easygoing adventurer everyone was familiar with. No, this was the man who pulled a knife and put it to her ribs in the space of a heartbeat. Her thoughts went to the stolen illuminated manuscript pages in her pocket.

Handsome Dan drew nearer, his body close to Azulea's. "I think you're the one who is closest to finding the truth. I think you will tell me."

Azulea scowled.

"Did you ever wonder why it is that traders travel the Labyrinth in groups? Or why the Market Guards do their patrols in no less than twos?" Dan didn't even wait for a reply. "Because it takes a team. There is more that can be accomplished working together. There is a greater chance for success in any endeavor."

"What does that have to do with me?" Azulea had had about enough of everyone lecturing her on what she should be doing.

"Because you're the only person in that whole cursed building who understands this," Dan snarled, and then the smile was back. "Please tell me what's going on."

"You think the 'please' makes a difference?"

"I can only hope." His tone was wheedling.

"My mother ran out to the graveyard. Amma was poisoned, not just with *Cinchona Aerium*, but with Corpse Bloom spores."

Handsome Dan caught her arm, stopping them both dead. The evening crowd swirled around them, ignorant of the drama taking place. He spat out a curse and tensed as if to run and then stopped. "But you're here." He leaned closer. "You know something."

Without meaning to, Azulea's hand went to the outside of her pocket, as if to assure herself the manuscript pages were still there. "I may have a clue." And perhaps—trader, smuggler, ne-er-do-well—Handsome Dan would have ideas on how to discover the thief.

Before she could say anything, there arose a commotion toward the edge of the souq. Shouts arose, followed by screams. There was a surge as people pushed past them in the other direction. Handsome Dan stepped in front, shielding Azulea's body from the press of the crowd as he craned to see.

"What is it?"

The shouts started to become clearer. "Revenant! Monster!"

Azulea sucked in a breath. They had misjudged the

timing. Her grandmother had already risen and made it to the souq. Her mother and Melehti had gone to the wrong place. Even now they were headed to an empty grave. "We have to stop the spores!"

Azulea ran toward the noise. She twisted and turned, trying to maneuver through the crowds. "When it reaches a large enough heat source, the body will explode, releasing the spores to infect hundreds more."

Azulea wasn't getting very far. It was like swimming upstream. Dan passed her and shoved his shirttail into her hands. "Hang on!"

He began violently pushing his way through the crowd. Where Azulea had tried to push, he bowled people over. He punched and kicked, and used his symbiote tentacle leg to literally throw people out of the way.

"Almost there," he gasped. And indeed, the crowd was thinning out.

Azulea felt the ground change from packed sand to cobblestone as they approached the central square to the souq. She could smell the spores. It was like a warm rot. It perfumed the air. "We need to contain it. A blanket, maybe. Something. Anything."

Dan grunted and jerked something from a nearby stall. He shoved it into Azulea's hands. "A rug."

"Perfect. Hurry."

He stopped. "Gods of hearth and hellfire."

Azulea shoved him forward. "It's not her. Ignore what you see."

Azulea tried not to imagine the spectacle: Her Amma standing there in the middle of the market square. Her clothing tattered and covered with dirt. Her flesh peeling, and from her head, the long stalk that oriented the Corpse Bloom's body, guiding it to city center.

"It's horrific."

Azulea lifted the rug. "She is dead. It is just a shell." She ran forward, holding the rug in front of her. Then Azulea felt the other side of the rug lift as Handsome Dan followed.

"A little to the left," Handsome Dan said through clenched jaws.

Azulea stumbled over a cobblestone but stayed on her feet.

"Now!" he yelled.

They crashed into a body. They both followed it to the ground, wrapping the rug around it. The corpse squelched and oozed unpleasantly. It was already decaying in the heat. This close, the stench was overwhelming.

The body swelled under the rug. Azulea closed her eyes and held her breath. There was a dull popping sound. The rug ballooned for a split second before settling down.

Silence.

"Did we stop it?" Azulea asked.

Handsome Dan coughed. "Ugh. I breathed some in."

"Don't be a baby. Are you old? Or infirm?" Azulea said impatiently. "*You* should be fine. Answer me. Did we stop *all* the spores?"

"Yes. I don't see the yellow spores anywhere but on the rug."

Azulea smiled. "Then we did it. A little medicated *kafur* and you'll be—"

And that was all she could get out before noise crashed in on them along with several Market guards and Melehti. And the Head Archivist. In fact, the entire square was suddenly filled with shouting and demands, and Azulea felt overwhelmed.

Melehti was there helping her up. Again. "Are you all right?"

"Yes," Azulea said, dusting herself off. Her body ached,

and her hands and face still tingled from the fire. *Was that just earlier today?* "Thank you. That was closer than I'd like."

"It was closer than *I'd* like," Melehti said.

Melehti's attention was behind Azulea. "Your mother cannot put off the Governor any more. Not after this. He will have demands. He will need assurances of the safety of the citizenry."

Azulea's mother was already talking to the people in the square, calming their fears. With half an ear, Azulea heard her offer assurances and promises to recompense anyone for damages. She was using every ounce of her personal charm. She was soothing an entire souq, bringing them down from panic to a shrewd haggling for compensation.

Azulea also heard Archivists and trainees scattered around the square, offering everyone still present medicated kafur just to be safe that no spores could take root.

Melehti ordered two of her guards to remove the body for burning outside the city.

"This is Archive business," Azulea's mother snapped, stepping away from her latest conversation. It was with the rugmaker. Somehow, in the space of a few minutes, she had convinced him he was the hero of the day. *Hero!* The Head Archivist explained that the excellent quality of his rugs had saved the city.

"We will take care of the body and bring her home," Azulea's mother added, her demeanor changing in an instant from Head Archivist speaking with a shaken community to grief-stricken daughter.

Melehti bristled. "Archive business. I'm really starting to dislike that phrase."

Azulea touched the other woman's arm. "She is right. No one has seen a Corpse Bloom in decades. We have the knowledge and the skills. If it weren't for Dan…"

Azulea paused. "Dan?" She shifted, first left, then right, seeking him, but Dan had disappeared.

"Handsome Dan?" Melehti clarified, rolling the words around in her mouth slowly. As if they tasted bad.

Azulea shook her head. "Never mind."

Melehti stilled.

Azulea could picture her lips compressed into a thin line of disapproval. Once again, Melehti felt she was being shut out.

"As you wish." Melehti summoned one of her officers. She whispered into his ear, and he ran off.

Azulea didn't want to ask. She had originally come down to the souq to find out more about how the manuscript pages came to be sold on the black market, but now everything had become so convoluted. Handsome Dan. Her grandmother. Azulea gulped, feeling grief well up in her chest. She tried to ignore the Archivists collecting Amma's remains and ensuring that no trace of the spore was left in the market.

She was exhausted and overwhelmed. Maybe she should just go home. She could begin again tomorrow. Azulea slid a hand in her pocket and swore. The pages were gone. She had no doubt as to what had happened. Handsome Dan had pickpocketed her.

The walk back to the Archive was silent and somber. The company of Archive staff, Hypatia, and Azulea, accompanied by Melehti and her small contingent of Market Guards, arrived to find the entire grounds ringed with soldiers. Azulea swallowed a groan. That was what Melehti had been doing.

"What's going on here?" demanded Azulea's mother.

A soldier approached and handed her a piece of paper. "Governor's orders, Head Archivist. They were very specific."

Azulea's mother scanned the page before crumpling it.

"What is it?" Azulea asked. She could already hear the questioning murmurs from the Archivists and trainees who accompanied them.

Melehti moved away from Azulea to join the soldiers. As if by silent signal, her guards jogged forward to the front doors of the Archive main building and entered.

Hypatia repeated the words from the missive. "The Governor has sealed the Archive. No one who enters is allowed to leave. For the safety of the Shining City," she added acerbically, before turning to Melehti. "The Archive has never been under the jurisdiction of the City, or the Governor, or any other petty political body."

"And the Archive has never had murder under its roof, nor allowed a dangerous artifact loose to attack the City," Melehti said.

"You overstep your bounds, Arbiter."

"You ignored the evidence that a dangerous killer roamed the Archive."

"You told her." Azulea's mother spun on her daughter and snarled in disbelief. "What I said was in private and in grief!"

Azulea fought the urge to cringe at the stinging rebuke in her mother's words. She straightened her shoulders. "I did."

"And I cannot ignore what just happened in the souq," Melehti continued. "Until we are convinced that it is safe, the Archive is be guarded. No one may enter or exit. Decide which side of the locked door you wish to be on."

The murmurs from the group of Archivists and trainees in front of the building rose in consternation.

"This is our home," was all Azulea's mother said before she strode forward, each step firm and forceful. She ignored the soldiers. The rest of the Archive personnel followed meekly.

As they came abreast of Melehti, Azulea's mother spoke so only they could hear. "This is not the end, Arbiter."

"No, it isn't," Melehti replied.

Azulea fought the urge to slap both of them. After what they had just witnessed, after the horrors of the day, and knowing there was still a killer at large, they chose to fight one another.

Inside, people headed to their various rooms and duties. Azulea did her best to not think about what the Archivists would do with Amma's remains. It wasn't long before it was just her, her mother, and Melehti trudging through the halls in an antagonistic haze.

"I need to talk to you." Azulea's words were abrupt as they arrived at her mother's office.

"You've talked enough," her mother snapped.

"No." It was one word. One small word but it was enough.

Her mother stopped.

"This is necessary."

Azulea could feel her mother wavering.

"Fine. If nothing else, your actions today in the souq tell me that your instincts are valid. But you, Arbiter, you can wait in the hall."

Azulea opened her mouth but then held her tongue. Now was not the time to push her mother. They were all too close to their breaking points.

The door closed, and Azulea heard the lock snick shut behind them. She turned and pulled at the door. It didn't budge. "Really, Mother?"

"Hmm?"

Her mother's half-distracted reply irritated Azulea.

"The door," she said tightly. "It isn't…" Azulea's words trailed off as she realized that room brightened and then dimmed. Her vision was enough to perceive light, and this wasn't normal. It pulsed and strobed.

"Mother?"

Azulea turned to her mother who stood frozen, staring at her desk. There was a flash of light and then another. Faster and faster.

Whatever it was, was bright. Even Azulea shied away from it. It floated just above the desk. She couldn't see much, but what light she did see was enough that the pulses of light shot pain straight to her temples.

The flashes got brighter and brighter and faster and faster. It began to whine. First in a low hum, then began to increase in pitch as it rose higher in the air.

Azulea shut her eyes and scrambled for the item. The side of her hand bumped a smooth globe. It was little bigger than an egg and cool to the touch. Its levitation disrupted, and it fell to the desk and rolled away from her desperate fingers as she tried to grasp it. She turned her head away as, even with her eyes closed, the pain from the flashes increased. Her stomach twisted with nausea.

It was a Lampyrid Strobe. Used to neutralize soldiers or to control crowds who had grown violent, it was a weapon from another world on the far side of the Labyrinth.

She heard it roll and fall with a clatter off the desk and bounce across the floor. No, no, no! Her mind filled with what she remembered of the Lampyrid Strobes.

Although easily triggered, Lampyrid Strobes have a limited time for flash frequency dependent on hertz level. At 10-12 Horus, a single strobe can last for up to thirty minutes. At damage-level intensity of 20-70 Horus, the strobes can only last a few minutes at most.

She heard a strangled sound from her mother before the dull thud of her body hitting the floor. Giving up her efforts to find the strobe, Azulea threw herself toward her mother. The high note coming from the strobe increased in pitch and volume again.

If the flash occurs equal to the blinks of vision (or evenly multiplied, $2*\pi*n/\omega$, where n is an integer and ω the angular frequency) the strobe's pulses will appear to not waver, but retain their strength and focus.

Her mother's heels drummed against the floor, and Azulea could feel her head slam back against the stone.

She held her hands over her mother's eyes, hoping that the seizure would stop. She shut her own eyes tight, but even through closed lids, the bright flashes came through. There was a roar of wet sound in her head that rose higher and higher. She gritted her teeth and screamed for Melehti.

Using the ocular nerves, the strobes can directly stimulate the brain. The strobing action will overwhelm the neurons causing multiple misfires, confusion, disorientation, seizures, bleeding, and eventually, coma and death.

In the background, Azulea could hear Melehti slam into the locked door over and over.

She smelled burning and began to cough. Under her, she felt her mother's body contract painfully before stilling. Her mother's breathing rushed in and out of her mouth loud and noisy, but steady.

There was a crash as the door gave way. Azulea could barely hear it as her own thoughts began to dim. There was the gentle tinkle of glass shattering, and then the room was dark. Melehti had found the strobe.

"It's okay, we've got you."

"Oh thank the hearth gods." She breathed before her stomach revolted. Azulea sat up and scuttled away from her mother and Melehti just in time to throw up. She hadn't eaten much today at all. She hunched over, gagging. Bile burned her throat, and her eyes watered.

"Um thrak, Archivisto."

It was Mosa. His words came from the direction of the doorway.

Azulea wiped her mouth and struggled to sit up. "Is she alive?"

"Shh, careful," Melehti said, a hand rubbing Azulea's back in a circular motion.

Azulea pulled away and reached toward her mother, her fingers coming to rest on her robe. She let them skim up the material to her arm, her shoulder, her neck, and face. She felt a flash of relief at her mother's even, though rapid, breathing.

"Thank you, Mosa," Melehti said. "I could never break the lock on my own. It is fortunate you were nearby."

"What happened?" Otha's penetrating voice came from the hall. "The guard, Mikkal, said someone was in the Head Archivist's office." She pushed forward and through the doorway, ignoring Mosa.

"I could not find the Superintendent," Mikkal said breathlessly from behind her.

"The Head Archivist…" was all Melehti could get out before there was a cry from the older woman. Otha rushed in and knelt over her sister.

"What happened?" she repeated, pulling back an eyelid and then tapping her sister's chest.

Azulea heard her mother stir. The movements were drowsy and lethargic. When Hypatia's stomach contracted, Otha and Azulea both gently held her as she vomited.

Melehti prowled the room, like one of the Namurian beasts from Old Mejeir's Bestiary. "Strobe. I couldn't tell what strength it was. The door was locked. We couldn't get into the office. Maybe five to six minutes of exposure."

"Notha ocus," Mosa said.

"What's wrong with my mother's eyes?" Azulea said after translating in her head, her concern rising.

"Bleeding. Probably nothing more than a side effect of whatever this did," Otha said deftly, using a corner of her robe to wipe Azulea's mother's mouth.

Hypatia tried to speak, the words raspy and confused. She was clearly disoriented.

Otha made soothing noises. She then called for Mikkal and the other Archive guards to carry Hypatia to the Infirmary. "I can better care for her there."

"I'll send more of my men to stand watch," Melehti said quickly.

"The Archive can…"

Melehti interrupted, her voice now coming from behind Azulea. "This was a trap, set for the Head Archivist. Whoever did this may try again."

"Oh," Otha said softly before changing her focus. "Azulea, are you all right?"

Azulea blinked. She was tired, and her head was pounding like the great bells in the tower clock. She tipped her head and grimaced at the bolt of pain. She felt someone kneel behind her, solid and warm. Melehti. The other woman's arms wrapped around her, keeping her steady.

"Yes. No. I don't know. My head hurts."

"Can you stand?" Melehti asked.

Azulea nodded and regretted the motion, nausea flaring.

"I've got you." Melehti pulled her to her feet with ease and held her close.

Azulea took a deep breath. Exhaled. Then she took another. The ground didn't quite feel quite so unstable.

Melehti said, "We should get them both to the Infirmary."

Azulea awoke slowly, her senses coming to life one by one. First it was the sound of birds and the rumblings of the souq. Then it was the softness of the bed under her. It wasn't the thin scratchy sheets of the Infirmary. She vaguely remembered demanding to rest in her own room. The warmth from the sun shining in from the window brightened the room from dark to a dull gray. Something moved beside the bed. Azulea gasped and sat up. Her head throbbed. She stretched her fingers. Her hands felt tight and hot from the burns.

"Azulea, I'm so glad you're all right." Peny grabbed her hand and held it to her, weeping noisily. Great wet tears poured onto Azulea's skin. "I thought you were going to die."

Azulea reached out and pulled her cousin onto the bed, hugging her tightly. "I'm fine. Just a headache." Her shoulder was getting damp. She patted Peny's back, ignoring the complaints from the cuts on her hand as the younger woman hiccupped and sniffed.

Azulea pulled back. "What time is it? How long have I been asleep?"

Peny hiccupped again and sniffed. "Late afternoon. Otha said to let you rest. Melehti would only leave when I promised to stay in her stead." Peny leaned forward and whispered conspiratorially, "Melehti's *very* worried about you."

"And my mother?" Azulea was afraid of the answer.

"She's alive. You saved her, you know," Peny said. "Otha gave her a draught, and they're keeping her in dark and quiet. She will recover."

"Seizure-induced temporary alterations in neural function include exhaustion, sensitivity to bright light and sound, the inability to think clearly, poor short-term memory, decreased verbal and interactive skills, and a variety of cognitive defects specific to individuals."

"Nothing wrong with your memory," Peny said cheerfully.

Azulea rubbed her hand over her face. She hadn't intended to say that aloud. "I need to see my mother." She inhaled and made a face. "And bathe. Again. I cannot lie in bed all day."

"I think you lying in bed all day sounds like an excellent idea," Melehti said, as she entered Azulea's room and sat down proprietarily on the other side of the bed.

"Don't you knock?" Azulea asked sourly, inexplicably irritated.

Melehti chuckled, unshaken by Azulea's crankiness. It was a vibration that rolled down her whole body. "I can see you are feeling more like yourself." She paused. "You are the one who asked me to stay," she added softly.

"I…" Azulea struggled for words.

Melehti's fingers played with Azulea's hair. "I just came to let you know that your mother has awakened. I thought you might like to see her."

"Hypatia, lay down, you'll injure yourself." Charemon's words were intended to be soothing, but Azulea couldn't help but feel a petty dislike toward the man. She had heard his questioning of her skills and abilities, and it was hard to let go. She stood just inside the doorway to the Infirmary. No one had noticed Azulea's presence yet.

"I must deal with the merchants." Hypatia's voice was weak but determined.

"You must take time for your mind and senses to heal." It was Otha. "If Azulea had not intervened when she did, your story might have ended very differently."

"The Governor will not wait. He has already sent a

summons." Hypatia's agitation had a jittery, palpable presence.

"I will go," said Charemon.

"That would be best, I think," said Otha.

"Do not talk about me as if I'm not here!" Hypatia's voice rose. It was edged with hysteria.

"Melehti's guards make it look like we cannot manage our own affairs." Charemon was defiant. "We must address this immediately."

Ashamed at listening in again, Azulea straightened her shoulders, pasted a smile on her face, and entered the room. She took a few steps toward the closest bed, stopping when her knees connected with the end of it.

She held up the tray of food. "I brought something for you to eat. Hashim in the kitchens grumbled that you should be eating Zharkhul eggs and cloven-hoofed Elasmoan entrails for strength."

"If that is what is under that cloth, you can take it right back down to…oh!" Otha exclaimed as Azulea removed the cloth, revealing simple bread and cheese with a bowl of broth on the tray.

"I didn't say I *let* him." Azulea's smile turned into a real one at her mother's laughter.

"We were discussing the summons from the Governor," Charemon said stiffly. "We must respond quickly."

"Yes, but my mother needs to eat," Azulea said firmly.

"Thank you, Charemon. We do not mean to be ungrateful," Hypatia said.

"Then it's settled," Otha said firmly. "While you are recovering, Charemon and the rest of us can make sure the Archive runs smoothly."

"And the investigation?" Azulea couldn't help but ask.

"You've certainly ensured that the Governor's pet will be addressing that issue," Charemon grumbled.

"Yes, I've ensured that someone will look into Amma's death, and for that I'm not ashamed!"

"Please. Charemon. Azulea," Hypatia said, her voice drained and thin.

"Enough! Everyone out," Otha said. "She needs to rest. Take your arguments out of here."

Azulea and Charemon were promptly ushered out, Otha quick on their heels.

He gave Otha an unhappy *hmm* before turning to Azulea. "We cannot let these attacks disrupt the Archive. When I visit the Governor, I think you should accompany me."

Azulea's eyes widened in surprise. "Me?"

"Close your mouth, you look like a fish." He *hmm'd* and muttered something about troublesome trainees, clearly referring to Azulea, as he headed down the hallway. "I will let you know when the appointment is made."

Azulea was glad she hadn't divulged that she'd lost the manuscript pages to Handsome Dan. Charemon would then have some very different things to say to her.

Azulea grabbed Otha's arm before she could shut the door to the Infirmary. "My mother will recover?" she asked quietly.

The other woman paused before answering. "I think so. But it will take many, many months."

Azulea felt her lips trembling and fought the urge to burst into tears like a child.

"It will be all right, Azulea." Otha pulled free and lifted Azulea's chin. "Very few people knew of Hypatia's childhood condition or how those flashes of light are more damaging to her than most, but she will get better. It'll just take time."

Azulea blinked. She hadn't remembered until Otha's words had reminded her of her mother's condition. The trap hadn't been random; it had been made specifically for her mother.

"What if the killer tries again?" Azulea asked. "They seem to know a great deal about the workings of the Archive."

"I won't leave her side," Otha said. "And, Melehti has scattered soldiers all around the Residence. Two of them are right over there in the far corner of the room."

"Thank you."

"No, Azulea. Thank you." Otha began to cry. "I love my sister very much. If you had not been there…you saved her."

≈

"I'm going to take another look at your mother's office," Melehti said. She walked right past where Azulea and Peny were seated in the Grand Parlor.

The room was still relatively busy, mostly with traders who were unable to leave the Archive but weren't willing to remain in their rooms. No warmth suffused the Parlor today. The broad doors leading out to the market were shuttered and under guard. The mood was somber with too much silence except for low murmurs of conversation.

Azulea was already grumpy. Handsome Dan was avoiding her. Every time she asked where he was, she was told that she had just missed him.

In addition, she and Peny had spent two hours going over the range in the Collections where the stolen illuminated pages had come from, trying to discover some pattern in the thefts and discern if they were related to the murders.

Azulea swiveled toward Melehti. "Not even going to ask, are you?" she said, acerbically. "It *is* a private office."

"No."

Azulea leapt to her feet. "I'm coming, too."

"But what about…" Peny said, half-heartedly.

"There's only one thing left to do." Azulea's words were quick. "We know that the pages focused on the Corpse

Bloom. Someone needs to go to the shelves in the Archive and see if there is anything left. Any sign from the thief. And murderer." She half turned, listening. She didn't want to let Melehti get too far ahead.

"I can do that!" Peny offered. "I know the section where it came from. It shouldn't be too far from the Parani scrolls. I'll find out about the Corpse Plague!"

"Shh!" Azulea hissed.

"Sorry," Peny said, only marginally quieter. Azulea half-ran out of the room. "And be careful!"

In the hallway right outside the Grand Parlor, Azulea paused.

"I waited."

Azulea hid her surprise. Melehti was usually much more impatient. "Thank you. Besides, it might be easier to get past Mikkal if you're going in with someone from the Archive."

Melehti snorted derisively.

They walked in companionable silence until they got to the opening that led to the back offices. Melehti, who was only a half of a step in front, stopped so quickly that Azulea ran into her.

"Wha…"

Azulea felt Melehti raise an arm, asking for quiet. Then she heard it. Faint snores. "You're kidding me. This was the kind of mercenary Charemon hired to protect the Archive?!"

She felt Melehti draw back. Then, the other woman lunged forward as she kicked out. There was a splintering sound followed by a crash and a yelp. She had kicked the chair out from under Mikkal, dumping the sleeping man on the stone floor. A moment later, his spear clattered to the floor beside him.

Mikkal scrambled to his feet. "I'm sorry. I'm so sorry. I didn't mean to. I was so tired. I…"

"Stop," Melehti said. Her words rang with command.

Mikkal's mouth shut so fast his teeth clicked together. She leaned forward. "A soldier does not sleep while on duty."

"I know. I'm sorry. I…"

"If you are too tired, either give your watch to someone else or walk the hall. Sitting is one step away from lying down, which is one step away from sleeping, which is one step away from dead. Do you understand me?"

"Yes. Yes, Arbiter. I won't do it again."

"I will hold you to that."

"Thank you, Arbiter."

Mikkal didn't even work for Melehti, yet he was already promising her his best effort. Azulea smiled. This was one of the reasons she had fallen in love with Melehti in the first place. She was firm, but always inspired loyalty and trust from those around her.

Stepping out from behind Melehti, Azulea offered Mikkal a smile. "We're going to investigate the Head Archivist's office. My mother," she reminded him.

"Of course. Yes. I hope she is well. Or doing well. Doing better. Go ahead. She's a great lady. Again, I am so, so sorry."

"Thank you," Azulea said with a regal nod toward the young man. She'd swear she heard him bow. The two women continued down the hall, leaving Mikkal and his continuing string of apologies in their wake. When it came to unending monologues, he was almost as bad as Peny.

"That man…" Melehti said.

"Don't say it," Azulea admonished.

"But…"

"I know."

There was a heavy sigh in response.

"I'm sure he will benefit greatly from having you and your soldiers around. Actually," Azulea's smile widened to a grin, "I should suggest that he talk to you about one-on-one lessons to improve his skills."

Melehti made a choked sound. "You are a cruel woman."

This time, it was Azulea who stopped. She put her arm out to the side, stopping Melehti.

The other woman was instantly on alert.

"What is it?"

She held a finger to her lips and glided forward, stopping outside the door to the Head Archivist's office. She pointed. Sounds came from within.

Melehti pushed past, and Azulea heard the other woman's hand on the doorknob. Then she felt a silent tapping on her arm. One. Two. Three!

They burst in. There was a muffled *oof* as Melehti charged and connected with the intruder. There was a thump as two bodies slammed into the heavy wooden desk.

"I have him," Melehti said grimly.

"I was doing nothing," Davarr trilled in his own language. His gills fluttered faintly before stopping with a choked sound. Melehti was leaning against his throat.

"What are you doing in here?" Azulea spat out the words. Rage suffused her. Was he the one? The man who had tried to kill her mother?

"There have been two deaths, an exposure to the Corpse Plague in the market, an attack on the Head Archivist, and here we find you in her office. Do you think we will just let you go?" Melehti growled as she leaned into the Elishian, his body bending backward over the desk.

Azulea sniffed. She was distracted by a faint musky odor that permeated the room. She took a step toward them both and inhaled deeply. Her brows snapped together in recognition. "You. You were with Garoq the morning of the fire."

There was a faint snick. Melehti had pulled her knife out.

"Why don't I ask you again?" Azulea said. She bared her teeth. "And if we don't like your answers, my girlfriend here will start carving little pieces out of your gills."

She had no intention of letting Melehti do such a thing, nor did she believe the other woman would be willing to, but in silent communication, Melehti quickly played along.

"You know my reputation, trader," Melehti growled. Her voice had dropped and was barely recognizable.

"Yes, yes," Davarr quickly agreed. "Angry Arbiter. Garoq was a friend."

At the skepticism on both of their faces, Davarr barreled forward with his explanation. "We met often. I bring him drinks from all the worlds."

"Why did you kill him?" Melehti's words were quick and sure.

"No, no. I did not kill him."

There was a squeal. Azulea suspected that Melehti was not being particularly careful with the knife.

Azulea's thoughts spun as she processed the information. "Wait." She put a hand out on Melehti's back. Melehti had the Elishian firmly pressed to the desk. The muscles on her back were tightly corded. There was no weakness there, no give.

"So you met with Garoq for alcohol?" Azulea repeated. "He would replicate them? Create a safer version?"

She heard a sound of assent.

"So that morning, you went to meet him," she prompted.

"I met with him, but he was too busy with some other project. So we tasted a couple of glasses. It was the sweetest blueberry gamay. So deep it was nearly black. It fluoresced with the glowing bacteria, flecks that looked like stardust." Davarr sighed and smacked his lips as if tasting the aforementioned drink.

"Then you just left?" Melehti asked, disbelieving.

"I left." Davarr's voice was starting to rise in anger. "I have done nothing wrong! I am a guest in the Residence; this is sanctuary ground."

He pushed forward, and Azulea winced as she heard his

body slam back against the desk. His head bounced against it a second later with a dull sound.

"Did he pay you?" Azulea asked suddenly.

There was silence. Melehti, she was certain, was surprised at the seemingly disconnected question, but she had a feeling Davarr knew exactly what she was asking about.

"We had a deal," the Elishian whined. "He said they were copies."

"Melehti, can you search him?"

There was a rustling followed by the sound of paper.

"It's a page from a manuscript," Melehti said, the pages crackling in her grip. "The Mathematical and Philosophical Principals of Al-Khwarizmi," she read aloud, sounding out the words carefully.

"You never struck me as someone interested in mathematics, Davarr," Azulea said cautiously.

Melehti seemed to have no doubts. "You're the one who has been selling the illuminated pages. You killed the matriarch."

"I killed no one. Davarr is not a murderer." Davarr's voice had risen in pitch, and he regressed to his own language.

"This is all the proof I need," Melehti sneered. The pages crunched in a way that made Azulea wince.

Azulea took a step closer and, speaking in Elishian, asked, "Davarr, why did you sell the pages in the souq?"

Silence greeted Azulea's question.

"You did not sell the manuscripts here in the Shining City, did you?" she said with certainty.

"I am not so stupid," Davarr said, his voice low, returning to Trade.

"What do you know of the Corpse Bloom?" Azulea asked. She purposely spoke in Davarr's native tongue. She didn't want to misunderstand.

"Very dangerous," he responded, his Elishian filled with dark notes.

"And how much would information about it be worth? What would you sell pages about the Corpse Bloom Plague for?"

Melehti huffed at being left out of the conversation, unable to understand their exchange. Azulea raised a hand asking for patience.

Davarr trilled a sound of confusion. "Nothing. Everyone knows about Corpse Bloom."

Azulea stepped out into the hallway and shouted for Mikkal. The young guard came at a run along with two of Melehti's soldiers.

"He's not our murderer," Azulea said to Melehti.

"Are you sure?" Melehti was unconvinced.

"Yes, I'll explain in a moment," Azulea said, inclining her head toward Mikkal and the guards. More and more, she was suspicious of everyone.

Melehti sighed but turned over Davarr to the soldiers and Mikkal, explaining his theft. Rather than wait for them to be done, Azulea wandered around her mother's office, her hands lightly brushing the various personal statues and artifacts that decorated the room. They were arguing as to whether Davarr should be held by the Archive's guards or by Melehti's City soldiers.

Azulea sat in her mother's chair. She had so many questions. How could they move forward? She was weary. She closed her eyes and let her senses reach out around her: The soft cushion of the chair, the wood of the desktop worn smooth by years of Archivists working at it, and surrounded by the space, Azulea noticed, just faintly, was the smell of her mother's perfume.

The guards withdrew, Davarr firmly in their grip. Mikkal's excited voice was still audible as they trudged away.

The door closed with a quiet thump, muffled by the thick woven rugs.

"Finally," Melehti said, coming around the desk. "What did you mean?"

Azulea opened her eyes. "The pages you returned to us talked about the Corpse Bloom. Davarr just said that the information about the Corpse Bloom is worthless. He wouldn't have taken it. He didn't take it, so it had to have been sold by the killer."

"The killer?" Melehti interrupted.

"I cannot believe we have two manuscript thieves at the same time. It would be too much of a coincidence. No," Azulea said firmly, "those pages were sold by Amma's killer. Davarr wasn't selling the pages he acquired from Garoq on this side of the Labyrinth. It was someone else."

"That is not proof. That is speculation."

"No, this is logic," Azulea argued. "Maybe they were hoping to confuse things or to blame him. Or even just to have information about the Corpse Bloom in the black market from a stolen Archive document at the same time there is an outbreak…"

Azulea could feel the wood flex under her fingertips as Melehti leaned back against the desk. The quiet between them was like the rivers during the monsoon season, flowing thick and fast but filled with so much debris. She could barely make out the shadow that was Melehti in front of her.

"So what do we do now?" Melehti asked.

The faint emphasis on the "we" caught Azulea's attention. Melehti was strong and confident and always unafraid. And sometimes a little—a lot—hot-headed. She was offering a partnership? Had she done that before when they were together? In her refusal to let herself lean on anyone, had Azulea been the one to destroy their relationship?

"I liked it, too," Azulea said, responding to the question

behind Melehti's words. "Working together. With you."

She took a deep breath and held out her unbandaged hand. Melehti caught it lightly.

"You called me your girlfriend," Melehti said, clearly delighted.

It was Melehti who had kissed Azulea the other day in her office. This time it was Azulea who pulled an unresisting Melehti to her and kissed her.

"I've been so caught up in proving myself, in being independent…"

"Caring about someone isn't a weakness," Melehti assured.

"Shut up," Azulea said, her lips still touching Melehti's. "I'm trying to apologize. It's not just sharing triumphs but also sharing burdens. I never allowed you to help me carry them. You're right, I didn't trust you. I couldn't control you. I was wrong, and if you'll have me, I'd like to apologize again, tomorrow. And the day after that."

Azulea could feel the other woman's smile against her own.

Melehti's arms enfolded Azulea, strong and dependable, yet still careful of her burns. "What about all the sunrises and sunsets that follow?"

Azulea leaned into Melehti's grasp and grinned. "I may have to think about that." The humor faded as did her smile as her mind came back to the present and their reason for being in the office.

Melehti released her as if sensing the moment was gone. "Well, we've solved one mystery, but we still don't know who the killer is." Her tone was pinched with frustration. Her fingers cracked as she balled them into fists.

Azulea dropped her own hands to her lap. Peny had helped her reapply the burn cream, but today they ached. "No, we don't, but we did learn something important."

"Amma's death was made to look like an accident. When Garoq was k-k-killed." She faltered but caught herself. She wasn't sure if she would ever be able to fully forgive herself for bringing him into her investigation. "When Garoq was killed, it was because he was analyzing the poison. There was no mistaking it was intentional."

"I don't understand."

Azulea plucked at the bandage on her left hand. It desperately needed changing. "Amma was killed, but it was made to be viewed as an accident so that she would have a great ceremony and be buried. But then, three days later, the Corpse Bloom Plague brought to the souq by the Mistress of the House of Books…that action was designed to cause problems for the Archive."

"And after the Archive is having problems with the community, if something were to take the Head Archivist out of commission…" Melehti continued.

"Then the Archive is in chaos."

"Which means…the thief, who is not Davarr, can steal more easily?" Melehti's voice rose at the end of her sentence. She wasn't sure she believed.

Azulea shook her head. "Davarr had a deal with Garoq. They must have been doing it for months. Look around. With all of Charemon's guards and security measures," she pointed to Melehti, "and the Governor's soldiers and his Arbiter prying into everyone's affairs? This would cause more problems, not less."

"But if Amma caught him—"

"He'd have killed her immediately, wouldn't he? That poison was from someone with a plan. They wanted not just to hurt her, or my mother, but to damage the workings of the Archive."

"And the reputation," Melehti added.

Azulea nodded. "Somewhat, but not seriously. Think

about it. Amma's spore-filled body was terrible, but not something anyone would believe that the Archive did purposefully. We were made to look the victim."

"You were made to look inept," Melehti corrected. She tapped her fingers against her knife hilt. "We are always a few steps behind this killer. I just don't see the plan."

Azulea felt a cold wave wash over her.

"What is it?" Melehti asked.

"The killer is following a careful strategy."

"Yes…" Melehti drew out the word.

"Except when someone is getting close to discovering information about their plan." Azulea grabbed Melehti and pulled her toward the door. "And Peny and I just announced in the Grand Parlor, loudly, that we would be examining the manuscripts where the Corpse Bloom information came from."

Melehti didn't say anything. She simply took the lead and ran, pulling Azulea behind her.

"Stupid, stupid, stupid," Azulea cursed. If she was the reason another friend died…her worry wrapped itself around her heart and squeezed.

"Left. Right. No, your other right," Azulea said exasperated. She and Melehti were winding their way through the Archive. Shelves and shelves of books and scrolls and parchments rose up to the ceiling several stories above. Narrow balconies followed around the room with ladders and stairs snaking through at odd angles and unexpected corners. But in spite of the seeming chaos and overwhelming collection, on each shelf, the items were all neatly stacked with tiny labels categorizing the contents.

"I can't see anything; it's too dim in here. And cold."

Melehti shuddered. She stepped aside and let Azulea take the lead.

"It keeps the documents from decaying," Azulea said, her steps sure and steady. She ran a hand idly along one shelf. "My grandmother walked me through every inch of the stacks. I didn't know it, but she was teaching me. I know from memory what is in each section and how to most easily find what people are looking for. I don't even need to use the Index."

Melehti's steps stuttered.

"What is it?" Azulea asked, her heart seeming to pause with her steps.

"You don't use the Index, so you would have gone straight to the location."

Azulea nodded.

"So maybe the sale of the manuscript was a trap," Melehti emphasized the last words to ensure her point sank in, "for you. Because you would go investigate."

Azulea didn't say anything. She only picked up her robes and began to run. "Four more shelves and then up. It should be on the third floor, second row back on the right."

Melehti quickly passed her. Azulea prayed that they were wrong and Peny would be busy researching. Even better, perhaps she was somewhere having an assignation. Never more did Azulea hope that her oversexed cousin had indulged.

She heard Melehti's nail-studded sandals run up the metal stairs and then clatter across the balcony to the upper rooms.

"Azulea! Hurry!"

Pulling herself up by the handrail, Azulea scrambled up the stairs. There was no mistaking the panic in Melehti's words. She turned right, passing the first set of shelves and then the second.

"I've found her." Melehti's voice came from the floor. Azulea dropped to her hands and knees. Pain lanced up her hands at the abuse. Even in the low light, she could make out the bright blond hair of her cousin. Melehti pulled her hands to a strip of material at Peny's throat.

"Strangled."

Azulea's fingers tugged at the stiff woven belt, her fingers scrabbling. "No, no, no." She was crying. This was Peny, her best friend. Her confidante. Her eyes.

"We're too late." Melehti's voice was leaden. "It must have only just happened. She's still warm."

"Help me," Azulea said through gritted teeth. Finally, the belt pulled free, and Azulea set it to the side. She put her fingers to the side of Peny's neck. It was slick with blood. Azulea could feel the gouges in her skin. Nothing.

"She put up a fight," Melehti observed. Azulea felt rather than saw her lift one of Peny's hands for closer examination.

Azulea violently slammed a fist onto Peny's chest.

Melehti jumped back, dropping Peny's hand. "Azulea!"

"Come on!" She put her fingers back at Peny's neck, ignoring the wet smears she caused. There! Just faintly, a pulse beat. "She's not gone yet." She reached over and placed Melehti's hand on Peny's chest. "Here. Keep rubbing in circles."

Azulea's mind raced as she tried to remember. "Come on. Think, Azulea." *Pressure on the windpipe of approximately 1/3 hundredweight is required to prevent ventilation. Death will occur in four to five minutes, if strangulation persists.*

She'd been muttering the words.

"That isn't helpful," Melehti said, mirroring Azulea's own distress.

"I know," Azulea snapped back.

She shook her head as more memories and statistics flowed through her mind faster and faster. She snatched at one. "Ibn Sina stated that a cannula of gold, silver, or another suitable material is advanced down the throat to support inspiration."

"What?"

"Never mind. Wait, get on top of her."

"What?" Melehti sounded stupefied.

"I need you to lie on top of her." Azulea repeated each word slowly. *"...and the child was dead and laid out upon the bed. He went up, lay upon the child, and put his mouth upon his mouth, sharing his breath. And the child became warm and was alive."*

Melehti positioned herself on Peny and pressed her lips to the other woman's. She blew. Nothing.

Azulea pinched Peny's nose closed. "Again."

Melehti did as she was told. "I can feel it. Her breath rises and falls."

"Good. Keep doing it." Azulea stood on shaky knees. "I must find Otha. She'll know what to do for an apneic state."

"Azulea, wait," Melehti said.

"Don't stop!"

"I won't, but take this."

Azulea felt Melehti's knife pressed into her hand.

"Whoever did this may still be near."

Azulea shoved the sheathed weapon into her pocket with a nod and ran. She didn't go back the way they had come. It would take too long. One of the most beautiful things about the Archive buildings was the arching stone bridges that connected several of the buildings that surrounded the square. She would take the stone bridge from the Archive Repository over to the main building and Infirmary.

Azulea slowed as she came to the hall leading to the bridge. She tended to avoid the bridges, for the obvious reason that she couldn't see the edges clearly and there was little for her to navigate by. That, and she just plain hated heights.

She heard a groan. Silhouetted by the daylight streaming in from the terrace was a crumpled figure. "Hello?"

"Azulea? What are you doing here?"

"Charemon?"

The old man struggled to get to his feet. Azulea tried to help him up. He wobbled and gripped her arm tightly. "Someone came through, running. They knocked me to the ground."

"Are you injured? We must get help. Peny was attacked!"

"Yes, yes. Of course, we must," he said, his hold tightening. "I don't want to slow you down."

They headed out onto the bridge. Azulea led, her steps were tentative. Charemon clung to her.

"I should have known better. I'm so sorry, Azulea." Charemon sounded pained. "I'd seen them earlier, you know. But with so many things happening at once…"

Azulea didn't stop moving forward, her free hand gripping the low wall so tightly she imagined she could feel every imperfection in the stone. "Who did you see?"

"It was Peny. She was with Mosa. They were talking. I just thought she was doing an interview."

Charemon was leaning on her more and more. He was not a light man. They moved slower and slower as Azulea struggled under the weight.

Azulea's heart started to beat rabbit-like in her chest. "Are you going to kill me now, or wait until we enter the Archive's main building?" she said through gritted teeth.

Her words elicited a guffaw from Charemon. "Azulea, you clever girl." Now both of his hands were wrapped around her arm, holding her securely to him. "What was it that gave me away?"

"I knew you were lying the moment you said you'd heard Peny and Mosa talking," Azulea said. "Mosa doesn't speak Trade, and Peny doesn't speak Lacerti."

She frantically listened for anyone—guards, soldiers, students—anyone below or around them, but there was no one. Should she scream?

"Languages were never my strength," he said dismissively. He released one hand to bring it to Azulea's throat. Her breath was suddenly trapped in her chest. He bent her back over the low stone wall. "It's why I never made Archivist. No, they picked your grandmother over me. And then your mother. It was supposed to be *my* turn."

Azulea kicked hard, pushing him back enough so that she could straighten up. She gasped and managed a quick breath before he was on her again. Frighteningly strong.

"And you."

Azulea could hear the snarl in Charemon's voice. "You had to interfere, so I had to make additional plans. A new tactic. But you wouldn't stop. Then you were helping Peny. And you just had to keep asking questions."

Azulea coughed and sucked in air. The puzzle was finally coming together. "You knew," she rasped. "I'd forgotten. But you knew. In the beginning, I only told two people that Garoq was testing the powder. My mother…and you."

"Then it will die with you."

"No one will believe…"

He took on a condescending tone. "A poor blind woman who, grief-laden at the events of the last few days, threw herself from the bridge. I saw her do it myself." He gave a mock sob. "There was nothing I could do."

Azulea gagged as his grip tightened on her throat again. Spots danced in front of her eyes. It wouldn't be long before she lost consciousness.

"Let her go!" Melehti shouted.

Azulea couldn't see her, but she could picture the other woman at the end of the bridge. And now, she could hear the pounding approach of Melehti's sandals on the stone.

Charemon yanked Azulea against his body. "Stop!"

Azulea tried to take a raspy breath, but his arm was still tight across her throat. She pulled at it weakly.

"I will break her neck." Charemon's voice rose.

Melehti's voice was a low rumble of sound. "Then I will break yours."

"No. You won't." Charemon stepped toward the side of the bridge, dragging Azulea with him.

Azulea struggled weakly.

"Not one more step!" he screeched.

Azulea felt Melehti's knife in her pocket. Melehti's knife. *No knowledge in the world will protect you from a knife between the ribs.* Azulea pulled it out and held it in front of her. Charemon couldn't see it, but Melehti would.

Azulea held up her fingers in silent signal. One, two, three!

Azulea swung her arm backward. She slammed the knife into Charemon's side. He screamed and released her. She fell to her knees. Not waiting, she crawled forward as fast as she could.

There was an angry bellow followed by a displacement of air and the pounding of Melehti's feet as she charged—a Mari enraged was nothing to trifle with. Azulea felt a faint tickle across her back before the thick sound of something connecting with Charemon. He screamed again, a short, sharp sound before there was a thud far below.

"Melehti?" she rasped as the booming steps drew close.

"I'm here." The Arbiter pulled her up and clasped her so tight that Azulea thought she'd never be able to get in a full breath.

"What..."

"I threw a spear at him," Melehti explained, tight lipped. "He went over the wall to the ground."

"Good," she said before burying her face in Melehti's

shoulder and sobbing.

※

It didn't take long to exchange stories. Peny had regained consciousness long enough to let Melehti know that Charemon was the perpetrator. After ensuring that Peny was stable and breathing relatively smoothly, Melehti had taken off after Azulea.

"I knew something was going to happen," Melehti said smugly. "I grabbed the spear from one of the shelves as I passed." She paused for a second. "Yes, you don't have to say it. I know. I destroyed one the Archive's priceless artifacts."

"I have no objections," Azulea murmured. She leaned into the warmth of Melehti's body beside her. Her hand was clasped tightly in Melehti's. They were in the Infirmary with Hypatia, Otha, Viera, and Peny as well as several of Melehti's guards. The sun had only just set, and Azulea could feel a cool breeze coming in the window.

Melehti finished, her words throaty with pride. "But Azulea had already rescued herself."

Azulea's smile was sad. "I'm sorry, Mother. I know Charemon was a close and trusted confidante."

Hypatia sighed. "He was your grandmother's cousin and had been a part of the Archive for so many years. I thought that a release from his duties would be a wonderful reward. I was wrong."

"Killing Amma wouldn't change anything," Otha said. "But he couldn't let go of the idea of being Head Archivist."

"I didn't realize anything," Peny added. "Well, not until it was too late." She sat on the edge of Hypatia's bed.

There were few outward signs of Peny's trauma, other than a dark bruise around her neck and the gouges where she had clawed at the braided belt, all of which was neatly hidden with Azulea's help. She had helped Peny pick the high-collared dress she wore.

"I'm so glad you are feeling better," Azulea said.

"I'm so glad you came to rescue me," Peny gushed in response.

Azulea wrapped her free arm around Peny's shoulders and gave her a quick squeeze. "Like you said, we're family. We take care of each other."

"I'll make my report to the Governor," Melehti said gruffly.

"Thank you." The words came from Viera. "It will take us some time to recover from the events of these past few days, but we are grateful."

"That doesn't mean we are giving up our independence," Otha added quickly.

"I understand," Melehti said.

"That means withdrawing your people," Otha pressed.

Melehti didn't answer.

Azulea suspected that this would be a new point of contention between the Governor and the Archive.

"But maybe some changes are in order," Hypatia said. Her voice was weak, yet firm. She was propped up on pillows. The meeting was held in the Infirmary out of respect for Hypatia's position, but already Otha and Viera and others were taking on duties to keep the Archive running.

"I may have been wrong about other things too...Azulea," her mother said softly, so only she could hear.

"If you are looking for Charemon's body, you will not find it." Melehti set the paper down. She and Azulea were seated side by side on Azulea's bed, knee to knee, thigh to thigh. It was now well into night, and they both had wanted nothing more than to go to sleep. However, it was impossible to miss the heavily perfumed note on crisp white paper that had been waiting for them in the middle of Azulea's bed. "Well, that explains the missing body."

Garoq's and Charemon's funerals were planned for tomorrow, but when the Archivists had gone to prepare the bodies earlier, they reported that only Garoq's remained.

Melehti kept reading. "I cut him into pieces and will feed him to the Selachii on the fourth day of Shomu."

Azulea touched a hand to her heart. The finned and toothed predators of the Laenite Gulf were vicious. The Selachii swam in packs and were known to joyfully hunt sailors and the ships that carried them through their dark oceans.

"I thought the gates to the Labyrinth were still closed."

"They are," Azulea said. Her voice was graveled with emotion. "I have no doubt Handsome Dan has a multitude of tricks to bypass our security."

"He's a Protistan slime mold," Melehti groused. "He also invited you to join him. He said he would hold back the best piece of Charemon for you to toss into the darkwaters."

Azulea turned her face away to hide a tear. Handsome Dan was a vain, violent, and unpredictable man, but in his strange way, he had loved her grandmother deeply. He did not get the opportunity to kill Charemon, but he would have his promised vengeance. "Does he say anything else?"

"He thanks you for the illuminated pages that garnered a lovely price."

Melehti stopped.

"Don't ask." Azulea waved her on.

"If you should ever choose some time away from your quest to be an Archivist, I would treasure your presence as a part of my trading caravan. My beautiful Zuzu—"

Silence.

"What?" Azulea asked.

"Do I really have to read this?" Melehti's voice was smoky.

Azulea laughed at Melehti's jealousy. "Go on."

"My beautiful Zuzu—"

"You read that part."

"Stop interrupting."

Azulea smothered another laugh behind her hand.

"There are many worlds out there, and your knowledge, your boldness, and your kindness are strength enough for any adventure. I will return. Until the Ancient One douses the sun from the sky, I remain your humble servant, Danislav."

Melehti folded the note. "That is quite an offer."

"Feeding Charemon's remains to the Selachii?"

"No," Melehti said humorlessly. "To join his caravan." She creased the paper carefully over and over.

Melehti's muscles twitched as she played with the note. She was clearly trying not to give her very strong opinion on what Handsome Dan could do with his offer. "So what are you going to do?"

Azulea beamed. For so long, she had been so focused on justifying that she could be an Archivist. She had been caught up in proving she was as good as anyone and everyone else, and in doing so, she had narrowed her world. She and Charemon had been alike in that way. But she didn't have to continue as he had. There was much more to life than just studies and stories and trade. There were so many options open to her…including a trip to the Laenite Gulf. All she had to do was open herself up to the possibilities.

"What am I going to do?" She wrapped a hand around one of Melehti's horns and pulled her in for a deep kiss. "Everything I want."

The End

ACKNOWLEDGMENTS

For a very long time, I was afraid to tell a story with a disabled protagonist of color. I thought no one would read it, no one would empathize with the character, or worse, she would be shelved away as one of those "special" books that are focused on educating rather than entertaining (not that I mind a little education). Therefore, I am grateful to Kate Marshall who pointed me to the call for writers and to Jaym Gates who thought the story idea was unique enough to encourage me to pull together the first 5,000 words (and then told me to write the rest). A multitude of thank yous to N. Renee Brown, Sherin Nicole, and Blythe Marshall who were my ever-patient team of Alpha Readers: I don't know what I would do without you. To Aaron and Angela Pound, Alisha Brown, Ginger Walker, Mindy Daniels, and Laura Henriksen...you guys are critique rockstars. And finally, I'd like to acknowledge the awesome team at Falstaff Books who helped bring this novella across the finish line: Jaym Gates, John Hartness, Melissa McArthur and Susan Roddey. It has been a grand adventure and this book owes every success to all these amazing people!

FALSTAFF BOOKS

**Want to know what's new
And coming soon from
Falstaff Books?**

Try This Free Ebook Sampler

https://www.instafreebie.com/free/bsZnl

**Follow the link.
Download the file.
Transfer to your e-reader, phone, tablet, watch, computer,
whatever.
Enjoy.**

ABOUT THE AUTHOR

Day Al-Mohamed is an author, filmmaker, and disability advisor. She is co-author of the novel *Baba Ali and the Clockwork Djinn*, editor of the anthology, *Trust & Treachery*, and is a regular host on Idobi Radio's *Geek Girl Riot* with an audience of more than 80,000 listeners. Her stories have appeared in Fireside Fiction, Apex Magazine, and Gray-Haven Comics.

She is a member of Women in Film and Video, a Docs in Progress Fellowship alumna, and a graduate of the VONA/Voices Writing Workshop. However, she is most proud of being invited to teach a workshop on storytelling at the White House in February 2016.

A disability policy executive with more than fifteen years of experience, she presents often on the representation of disability in media. She lives in Washington DC with her wife, N.R. Brown. You can find her online at DayAlMohamed.com and on Twitter @DayAlMohamed.

Printed in Great Britain
by Amazon